No Surrender

A novel by
DALE LUCAS

Published 2013 by Beating Windward Press LLC

For contact information, please visit:
www.BeatingWindward.com

Text Copyright © Dale Lucas, 2013
All Rights Reserved
Book & Cover Design: Copyright © KP Creative, 2013
Cover Artwork by: CJ Hutchenson & Red Statyk
Author Photo by J. P. Wright

First Edition
ISBN: 978-1-940761-00-8

Also by Dale Lucas

Doc Voodoo: Aces & Eights
Doc Voodoo: Crossfire
Right Behind You (E-Book Story Collection)

1

I am an old man, and I shan't be long for this world. Mortality has a way of forcing one to re-examine assumptions about oneself and I am left with no more justifications for my actions. I am a killer, a murderer—perhaps even a fiend, for more than once the act of taking lives filled me with a sense of grim satisfaction. But you must believe me when I say that every crime I perpetrated was undertaken in the name of justice, in the name of mercy, in the name of hope.

Nonetheless, now I realize that fighting a monstrous evil made me monstrous. That, I think, is the Dark Man's final jest upon me. I did all the wrong things for all the right reasons, just as he planned. What I did was not done in the name of the United States government, nor goodness nor decency. It was not done for racial equality, nor for political gain. No, what I did was done in the name of rage, in the name of hatred, in the names of men I had served with who died horrid deaths at the hands of men in white robes, who prayed to vile gods. What I did was done in the name of terror and the name of revenge, pure and simple.

Let this be not simply a confession, then, but a sort of instruction. I should like you to learn from my mistakes, if you can. If you dare.

I joined the Army in Rhode Island, fought in Tennessee and Georgia, but ultimately found myself commanding a detachment of peacekeeping troops stationed at Fort Brooke in Tampa, Florida. If you've never been to Tampa, let me describe it for you—at least, as I remember it in those days. I hear the city has done well for itself since our troops, bound for Cuba, were shuttled through there in '98, but back when I was there—I think we arrived in May of '65—Tampa was a dirty, slipshod little backwater that had gone to ruin since most of its inhabitants either left to fight for the Confederacy or abandoned the township for their farms in the countryside. Its sweltering streets were dusty, rife with crabgrass and sandbur, while its emporiums, houses, hotels and saloons were all in need of repairs and fresh coats of paint. The bright, merciless Florida sun coupled with the bay's turgid humidity and frequent summer rains made of the little burg a festering, malarial swamp, a haven for mosquitoes and cockroaches, attended by slithering serpents and the occasional obstreperous alligator. There was little to do thereabouts but drink, gamble, fan oneself, and grouse about the climate. I tried, in the early days of our arrival, to keep my men drilled, but after a few weeks I realized it was pointless to keep them marching, putting on daily parades in their hot wool uniforms under that imperious sun. So, discipline fell by the wayside and my entire unit joined the locals in their somnolent daily pursuits. I'm not proud of this, mind you, but I swear, there was little else we could do.

From time to time, we undertook policing actions per our mandate, responding to calls for aid from harried Freedmen's Bureau representatives or needy negroes in the wilderness suffering at the hands of local farmers. We were spat upon by farm wives and called nigger-lovers; we were threatened by scowling crackers with missing teeth and louse-infested beards; and at least twice a day some poor, sodden Johnny Reb back from the war less an arm or a leg would pronounce us Billy Yanks or blue-coated cowards, then challenge us to duels. We met all of these challenges with lazy indifference or blunt force, depending on our mood and the time of day. Generally speaking, we kept the peace that we had been sent to keep, and spent the rest of our waking hours sweaty, sullen, and bored.

The upset to our apple cart came in the autumn of '68, just as the weather seemed to be cooling and the clouds of mosquitoes thinning. I was at ease that balmy evening in one of the city's saloons, nursing a bottle of rum and a cheap cigar. A peddler from up north—a swarthy fellow with regal bearing and a salacious grin—was treating myself and the other patrons to a magic lantern show, projecting battlefield photos on a tacked-up sheet as the shabby moll that traveled with him sang 'The Battle Hymn of the Republic' to the accompaniment of an out-of-tune piano. More than one patron had already left the saloon, finding the charnel chiaroscuros of the peddler's picture show disagreeable. But I—having seen so much carnage first hand that I had become inured to it, if not a little enamored of it—I was going nowhere.

"Those rebellious sons of whores," the peddler muttered as he slowly, rhythmically changed the pictures in the aperture. I was sitting nearby him, and I think he knew I'd be sympathetic to his quiet rebukes.

"Sons of whores, indeed," I said, studying a crisp black and white image of a Union private, dead in a ditch.

"If only we could make each and every one of them—man, woman and child—pay for the blood they spilt… the bloody chaos they loosed…"

Though he claimed to be nothing more than a traveling salesman—his specialty being magic lanterns, stereoscopes, and daguerreotypes of war photography—he spoke with the cadence and authority of a Shakespearean actor. His manner of speech, his great height, and his darksome, Old World complexion all combined to give him a strangely noble bearing—nobility not being one of the most common attributes among roving peddlers.

I was under the man's spell at that moment, in more ways than even I realized at the time.

Then one of my subordinates burst into the saloon and hurried to my elbow, and the spell was broken.

It was Cabott, a wide-eyed, lantern-jawed private from Vermont, who desperately sought my attention. He threw me a quick salute, then quickly spat out the reason for his interruption of my evening's entertainment.

"Lieutenant Kenning!" he said. "Come quickly, sir! There's a man in the barracks! He stumbled in from the countryside and he's stark raving mad!"

Stark raving mad sounded like a welcome interruption to the monotony of duty in Tampa, so I excused myself from the magic lantern show and let Private Cabott lead me back through the mosquito-infested night to our barracks on Whiting Street. On the way, the private gave me some scattered, disjointed details culled from the affrighted newcomer, but I paid little attention. I was determined to see the man for myself and make my own judgment as to his relative sanity.

The barracks were, in peace time, a warehouse for goods arriving at the city's fetid little port. The air was close within and the building smelled of sweat and sawdust. My men were all gathered round a particular bed, by which stood my sergeant, Mulvaney, who was engaged in asking the occupier of the bed some questions. I made a point of clearing my throat to announce my arrival, and some semblance of order was instantly restored. Mulvaney urged the soldiers to withdraw and stand at attention with a silent glare. They did as commanded. The fellow in the bed—our erstwhile guest—saw that I was someone of stature and fell silent as well. I didn't like the way his feverish gaze seemed to both plead with and accuse me all at once.

The fellow was, indeed, stark raving mad. For one thing, he wore a raggedy white robe, torn and dirtied by his passage through woods and palmetto scrub. For another, he was clearly hungry, mad with thirst, and whittled down to skin and bone. I greeted him, telling him who I was and asking just what he'd come to us for. I almost asked him just what he was doing in those tattered, filthy robes as well, but decided the truth would probably come out soon enough. The bony, pop-eyed fellow did his best to stay calm, but I could see he was having a hard time of it. He begged for a drink of water. After I gave him some, he began his story.

The preface to his tale was fragmented, but this was the gist of it: his name was Yates, and he was from Calusa County, a region directly south of Tampa and the bay that stretched all the way to Okeechobee and the Everglades. Yates, it seems, was a well-to-do farmer in that region—not a rich plantation owner, mind you, but still a respectable yeoman with good acreage and some money in the bank. Like most of the able-bodied men of Calusa County—and Florida, for that matter—he had gone to war and left his family behind to tend the farm. War had its way with him— as it had with all of us—but he'd come home with all his limbs intact and only his pride and his sense of the sanctity of life shattered. He returned to an untended farm, because his wife and sons had all succumbed to one of the region's frequent yellow fever outbreaks.

"So, you see," he said, after rambling through his narrative and making frequent and often confusing digressions, "I came home to nothing, with nothing. A broken man in a broken world."

I understood his melancholy. We all suffered some form of it. I still had frequent nightmares about the men I'd seen torn to shreds by cannon fire and pierced by musket balls on the fields at Stones River and Chickamauga. I dealt with my distemper like most men did—by talking about it as little as possible and drinking regularly to keep the demons at bay. That prescription seemed to be working, so I saw no fault in it.

"But what's this about?" I urged, growing impatient. It had taken the man almost an hour of babbling to tell me who he was, where he was from, and that he was a widower. "It looks like you've gone to hell and back just to bring us some news, so I think you need to spit it out."

That's when he looked very grave, his eyes growing wide and his mouth turning down sorrowfully. I thought at first it might be fear, or just exhaustion, but then I realized it was something else entirely.

Shame.

"The things we did," he suddenly sobbed, breaking down there in front of me like a child. "Oh, sweet Jesus, sir—the things we did! When I saw him—when I saw him, I knew I had to tell someone. I knew that it would only get worse."

I was intrigued, I'll admit, but I needed him to start making sense.

"See here," I said, scooting a chair closer to him and taking a seat, "I need you to be clear. What is it you did, and who did you do it with? And, perhaps most importantly, why do we need to know about it?"

He leaned closer and whispered conspiratorially. "Because," he said, with a gravity that frightened me, "if you don't act quickly, sir, it could be the end of everything."

He had my attention.

2

He was not alone (he told us) in coming home from the war with wounded pride to a broken home. Many of his closest neighbors and brothers-in-arms suffered the same fate, nursed the same spiritual wounds, and knew the same grief. His good friend Lyle Beresford, for instance, was reported dead, and so his wife had remarried and already borne a child with a sugar cane planter who had been given a dispensation against the Confederate draft. Another farmer, Carver, had lost his wife to highwaymen taking advantage of the chaos left in the wake of so many men running off to fight for their would-be country. One fellow's grocery business had fallen under the shadow of a rival's dry goods business and failed. But none of them seemed to be so hurt by the Confederacy's loss, so haunted by their broken dream of freedom from the Union, so humiliated by their surrender, than one of Yates's oldest and dearest friends, the scion of a wealthy and respected planter family that made their home at the handsome plantation grounds known as Bellhaven, down in southeast Calusa: Orion Bell.

Orion Bell was a young man of courage and means. When he rode off to war on his best horse, he left behind an elderly but still vital father—Josiah Bell—and a hopeful, spirited sister who was just shy of marrying age—Livia. The way Yates talked of this Bell, it was clear the young man was the leader of his respective pack—first to volunteer for hazardous duty, first to put spur to flank and send his mare charging heedlessly into the thick of battle, first to seek the company of women or to throw his money in the pot for a communal bottle of liquor. Orion Bell, therefore, was nothing less than the living embodiment of all the hopes and dreams of the many young men who answered their country's call to arms and left hearth and home to fight for their beliefs. That fact made poor Bell's misfortunes upon their return all the more poignant.

Bell, Yates informed us, had been present at Appomattox when Lee surrendered, and carried the memory of that dark day all the way home with him. He considered that surrender an act of betrayal on Lee's part, and the fact that the Confederacy had stopped fighting—even when some of its cabinet members could still have escaped to Cuba or the western territories—a gross dereliction of duty. He and his companions from Calusa County traveled home as a band of broken men, moving across the burned and blighted landscape of the now done-for Old South, reminded at every turn of what might have been, and what never would be.

But their homeward march was nothing compared to what they all came home to. The misfortunes of the others I've already related, but Bell's own stature as the most blessed and privileged of that company meant that his personal fall from grace—his personal hell—would be far more moving and heart-breaking than that of any known to his farming and shop-keeping fellows.

When Orion Bell returned to Bellhaven, he returned not to a warm and welcoming ancestral home, to the arms of a proud father and a sympathetic sister, but to a bedeviled ruin already in danger of being reclaimed by the local flora and fauna, and plantation lands that had not been worked or maintained properly for years. His sister, Livia, had gone mad in his absence—broken-hearted over the loss of a male suitor whom she had planned to marry at the war's close. Said suitor surrendered his head to a cannonball at Gettysburg, and since the news had reached poor Livia, she had been a broken woman. By Yates's report, Orion Bell found Livia wandering the corridors of their ill-kept plantation house, wearing a yellowed, grimy wedding dress that she would now never have use for, babbling to herself incoherently and collecting bundles of dandelion and skullcap from the yard. Adding to her grief over her would-be suitor, Livia had also found old Josiah Bell, her father, dead as Julius Caesar one morning, hanging from a rafter in his personal library with a blue face and a swollen, lolling tongue. He had, apparently, hung himself in the night when he realized that his country's cause was hopeless, and that the life the Bells had always known—a life of pride and leisure and lordship—was at an end. Adding insult to injury, Orion Bell found the negroes of his plantation—normally so hard-working, so tractable that the whip was seldom employed to motivate them—had all revolted and formed a number of little villages on plantation lands. They administered themselves now, and the few crops currently raised on Bell's ancestral soil were everyday staples raised by these ungrateful darkies for their own subsistence. Yates reported that Bell had, apparently, tried to rally the blacks to take to the fields once more and help him plant and bring in a cotton crop—for even the Union would still need cotton, war or not—but the brutes refused him, saying they were no longer his property and, begging his pardon, they would no longer do his bidding without wages. Had Bell's fearsome old overseer, Milo, been at hand, Bell might have unleashed the brute as he would a brace of hungry, snapping hounds… but alas, Milo had run away when his master, old Josiah Bell, hung himself.

Thus did Orion Bell, once the scion of a proud family and the inheritor of a vast tract of well-worked land return from war to find his family shattered, his lands gone to ruin, his pride stripped, beaten and spat upon.

Yates's sympathy for his old compatriot was clear, for as he told this tale, he summoned tears for poor, unhappy, suicidal Josiah and lamented lovely Livia's madness as though she were his very own sister. Bell's fall from grace seemed to represent for Yates and all their companions the collective fall they had all endured, but with an outcome more bitter, turns of fate more terrible, than any of the rest of them had ever known or imagined. Yates's sympathies dried up, however, when he reached the point in his tale whereat Orion Bell decided to have his revenge, by any means necessary.

As the world around him changed—as Radical Republicans replaced the men he had known all his life in local and state-level politics, as scalawags and carpet-baggers swept down from the north like locusts to feed on the derelict produce of the fallen South, as Freedman's Bureau representatives combed the countryside to organize and enfranchise the now-manumitted negro populace—Orion Bell retreated into the shadows of his family home and undertook dark, even blasphemous researches into orders and powers beyond the mundane, seeking into the dark corners of man's occult knowledge for some means of restoring the glory of the South, and by extension, his own rightful place as the proud scion of a powerful family on a prodigious estate.

Old Josiah Bell had, Yates told us, been quite the collector of arcane and esoteric volumes, although he had always done so simply for the sake of owning a rare commodity, and shown no special interest in occult knowledge. Now, his son drew all those volumes down from their dusty shelves, cracked their hand-bound old spines, and set to work perusing their contents in search of… well, Yates admitted that he didn't know what, precisely, Bell was in search of. Yates was no scholar, but he'd heard many stories in his lifetime and was both literate and no fool. When he called on Bell and always found him lost in study with all manner of strange and ancient tomes—from the *Book of Soyga*, thought long-lost from the library of the infamous Doctor Dee, to the blighted *De Vermis Mysteriis*, and even including the dread *Necronomicon of the Mad Arab Abdul Alhazred*—he knew that he should worry. These were not idle researches, he suspected, but vile obsessions that could ultimately lead his friend—and perhaps his entire community—down a road that spiraled into the deepest, darkest abysses of human depravity.

More than once, Yates and his boon companions about the county tried to warn Bell that he was crossing lines best not crossed, daring insights best not dared, lest he end up a mad and drooling lunatic, even farther gone than his dear, insane sister (who now lived in an upstairs room of the family home and had her everyday needs attended to by her embittered sibling). But Bell would hear none of it.

"Somewhere in all this moldy old knowledge," Bell assured the terrified Yates, "lies the secret to our redemption—the means by which we shall be revenged upon those scoundrels and villains in blue who dared to invade our homeland and tear down our revered institutions. Weapons of fire and steel have failed us, it's true—but there are other weapons that men can use upon one another—some of them from realms beyond our everyday ken, handed down by the gods themselves. If the God of my forefathers has so rudely failed us in our hour of need, then I shall turn my back on Him gladly and seek satisfaction elsewhere, with other sponsors, be they wicked, or cruel, or even, ultimately, daemoniac in nature."

I must admit that, at this point in Yates's tale, I was starting to have some sympathy for the obsessive Orion Bell. True, I thought his way of life shamefully Old World and his country's dedication to the peculiar institution of slavery abhorrent, but I knew what it was like to feel abandoned by God—to wonder if any deity at all listened to the idle prayers we offered, or if that deity and its unseen fellows were, perhaps, just a little mad. I saw little of God on the battlefield, less in the war's aftermath. Feeling so abandoned, why shouldn't a man seek satisfaction, or even some solace, in strange rites and worships? Thus, I urged Yates to carry on with his tale.

Yates tried to speak with his fellows about Bell and his studies, but none of them seemed concerned. A few baldly disbelieved him. In time, he convinced himself that Bell was, perhaps, just on a bit of a tear, emboldened by grief and bitterness. Though lost in somber esoterica at the moment, Yates reasoned Orion Bell would find his way back to solid earth in time and leave his devilish studies behind. And so, for some months, he left him to his researches.

An opportunity to ground Bell came when the white men of that district started to note a change in the hitherto cowed and deferential behaviors of the blacks that had once been their slaves. Calusa County was an underdeveloped backwater, and as such, had not attracted large numbers of carpet-baggers or Republican reformers as yet, but enough had passed through the region to energize the local freedmen with promises of voting rights, parcels of land, free education and paid labor. Now, to Bell and Yates and the men like them who had come home so humiliated and beaten, it seemed that even their God-given supremacy over these dark brutes was to be challenged. Stories made rounds in the county about black men whistling at or accosting white women; about black children daring to speak with white children who were clearly their betters; or white men challenged on the road by negroes in search of coin or trade goods or tack for their own horses and mules. In short, the world had turned upside down, and Calusa County was far enough from Tampa and the nearest garrison of soldiers that no enforced order was forthcoming.

(I had to hold my tongue all through Yates's vile ramblings about the humiliations that good white folk had to endure at the hands of 'uppity niggers.' In my part of the world, it's a simply understood fact that black folk and white folk, beyond the colors of their skin and the particulars of their everyday culture, are in every other way equal. Hearing this man—who'd already been beaten in a war to prove that very fact—still speak of the dark folk of his home county as chattel… well, all I can say is, it tried what little sympathy I had summoned for him in his madness and distress. Here, then, was the root of my eventual sin, to see that ruined, humiliated, bedeviled man as somehow fundamentally inferior to myself…)

Faced with a lack of order and eager for a fight, the men of that corner of Calusa County decided that something must be done, and that they were the very hands to do it. They went to Orion Bell, hoping to draw him out of his grim researches with their many reports of racial unrest in their neighborhood, and, by Yates's reckoning, they succeeded.

"Well, then," Bell proclaimed to his distressed fellows, "if our betters in blue will leave us to be so abused by those who once picked our cotton and hacked our cane, we shall just have to fend for ourselves."

And that's precisely what they did.

It was at this point in his tale that Yates—slowly but surely seeming to regain his sense as he told his story—took handfuls of the ragged white robes that he wore and displayed the raiment for us.

"This is what we wore," he said. "These were our uniforms."

"Uniforms for what?" I asked.

"Peacekeeping," he said, with a mad grin that I didn't relish. Then, his downtrodden mood returned and he lowered his eyes. "We thought we were just doing our part to keep order. To defend our little corner of the county from the depredations of those brutes. Although we went to Bell to draw him into our circle, upon hearing of the troubles, he seemed to have a plan ready at hand. It was his idea to wear these robes, and the masks. It was his idea that we should be not just a militia, but a secret and sworn brotherhood, complete with oaths and bylaws. He became our Grand Wizard, and we his minions. It was his idea to ride by night, to use fire and terror and the whip to instill fear, and when fear didn't work, to... to..."

"To what?" I urged.

"We never imagined that he had other purposes," Yates assured me with a shaking head. "We never knew that the robes were part of some blasphemous rites... or that the hangings were sacrifices."

No, he assured us, they had not known these things when they began. At first, they would ride out, several nights of the week, clad in their flowing robes and peaked caps and masks (all fashioned from bed linens, curtains and the like). They would visit the black settlements and terrorize them without let or hindrance. They would set fire to corn cribs and chicken coops, trample gardens and burn their produce, even engage in direct and violent confrontation when challenged. Mouthy bucks were beaten or shot; resistant women were ravaged and left with their clothes torn and their flesh exposed. When they received word of some specific transgression by one of their former slaves, they would find the man in question, cull him from any friends or neighbors who could come to his defense, then spirit him away to the cypress swamps for an impromptu trial and summary judgment.

"There have to be dozens of them in those swamps by now," Yates mused, as though just now realizing the full extent of his sin, "Frightened men hung from live oaks and slash pines, their lives choked off at the end of hemp ropes, their bodies left for the buzzards and crows."

But, Yates assured us, that was not the worst that he and his cohorts were guilty of. No, insult was added to mortal injury by the fact that, soon after they had embarked on this course of terror and conspiratorial murder, Orion Bell began to orchestrate every execution in such a manner as to make it a ceremony... a blasphemous rite dedicating the many men they hung to some ancient, unknown demon from the pit with a name that Yates himself could barely pronounce, though he had heard that name on Bell's lips hundreds of times.

"Nyarlathotep," he said slowly, lowering his eyes in shame. "I never heard such a name, not in all my life..."

Yates had hoped that when the other men saw evidence of Bell's blasphemies and spiritual decadence—when they saw, at last, that what he prized was not order but madness—they would turn against him, or, at the very least, try to talk sense to him. But, alas, it was not to be. Only Yates seemed to have any misgivings about the frightful rituals that attended their moonlight raids. The rest, instead of shunning and rebuking Bell, seemed to see him as some strange messiah figure—a holy, fiery prophet to be revered and supported without question, no matter what paths he led them down, no matter what damnation he brought upon them.

Bell, for his part, reveled in his new role. He would gather the men and take them out every night of the week. At least two to three times in each week, they would take victims to the cimmerian glades of Big Cypress swamp, say their unholy rites over them, then hang them from the stoutest bough and watch them dance their last jig in a noose.

"What was he after?" I asked at a quiet moment in Yates's narrative. "What did he hope to gain with all these rites and rituals, these dedications to strange old gods?"

"He hoped to catch the Dark One's attention," Yates said simply, as though it were the simplest thing in the world to see. "Every death perpetrated in his name—in that vile and blasphemous name—was a gift. Bell thought that once sufficient gifts had been given, the god would come to him."

"Fat chance," I scoffed, disgusted by Bell's apparent foolishness and wastefulness with human life. I poked a finger at Yates. "If Christ himself didn't intervene while we were all fighting and dying and calling his name in our wars, what made Bell think he could do any better with a god whose name hardly anyone knows?"

"I don't know what he was thinking," Yates admitted. "But he was right, sir. One night, after stringing up a scared young buck who'd pleaded for his life and promised to leave the county and never come back—right after that boy was hefted and hung and pissed his pants and rattled his last, it happened."

I waited. Yates said nothing. "What happened?" I finally asked.

"The god came," Yates said.

This is how Yates described it: he and his fellows were all standing around in a circle, as they had any number of times before, watching their victim's body sway where it hung. There was a full moon that night and the sky was clear, so they moved in the marsh without torches, the moonlight being sufficient to illuminate their grim work. A breeze slithered with serpentine ease through the cypresses and Spanish moss, whispering prayerfully in answer to the death throes of that boy they'd strung up, and all through the swamp the native sounds of trilling insects, croaking frogs and hooting owls filled the air like the babble of a crowd in a closed room.

And then, without warning, all those beastly and familiar sounds from the swamp ceased. Yates swore that he had not known it was so loud until there was no sound at all. Not a bug buzzed, not an owl hooted, not a bullfrog croaked. There was only the sough of the breeze in the bog pines, and somewhere, not too far off, the sound of someone—or something—moving through the watery sloughs of the marsh.

The sudden silence and the sound of that dread approach moved all the men to arms. They spent only an instant meeting one another's frantic gazes in the moonlit murk, then scurried to their horses for their rifles or drew up their robes to get at the guns holstered on their hips. Some of them, according to Yates, thought that the law might have finally found them out—a Republican sheriff or a military unit like my own—but Yates himself and many of the others knew the truth: the sound they heard, some great body moving with deliberate slowness through the deep muck and underbrush of the holm, was not the sound of a band of lawmen or even a hapless convocation of negroes taking a shortcut home from some adjacent settlement. No, it was a single entity—something large that moved inexorably toward them with every passing moment.

The wind increased then. The pines susurrated and the cypresses creaked and the beards of Spanish moss on all the trees whipped in the wind like tattered banners above a decimated regiment. In the midst of that howling, rising wind, the men all shrank together into a large knot in the center of the glade. They cocked their hammers and raised their sabers and peered into the darkness to see what was upon them. They searched all sides, for with the rising wind, they could no longer tell where their attacker approached from. Only Orion Bell stood apart, on guard, pistol in his hand, but confident, more curious than cowardly.

Then the wind stopped.

"There he stood," Yates told us, eyes growing wide as a pair of side by side pocket watches. "Just at the edge of the glade, under the shade of the trees. He was taller than any of us—seven feet, eight!—and save for his broad shoulders and narrow hips and long arms and grasping hands, we could make out nothing clearly about him. He was darkness incarnate, a shadow with substance. Just looking on him made me cold, a cold that penetrated deep into me, to my very soul."

"Did he speak?" Mulvaney asked.

"Worse," Yates said, his whole body shaking, that look of shame returning to his eyes. "He put pictures in our minds—pictures of the things we'd done, and of the things he would help us to do."

Yates did his damnedest to describe these pictures, but his madness and growing agitation rendered his attempts almost incomprehensible. Suffice to say, the Dark Man in the glade seemed to fill their minds (if Yates's tale was to be believed) with the vilest and most terrible transgressions imaginable. The way Yates told it, every man was shown an image in his mind, like a waking dream, of himself as the most fearsome, felonious, ferocious beast in the whole of Calusa County. In these belligerent, bestial incarnations they saw themselves raining terror and destruction down upon their enemies. They were treated to images of rape and pillage, of murder and dismemberment, of child sacrifice and of human flesh partaken of as both sacrament and sustenance. When the storm of images and the waking dreams passed, the men could see the Dark One standing there at the edge of the glade, arms outstretched generously, a vile god offering viler rewards for their allegiance.

Orion Bell stepped forward, opening his own arms, eager to embrace that foul apparition like a long-lost companion.

That was when Yates broke from the company and ran.

"I stole a horse," he said. "They were all so awe-struck, so terrified and amazed that they didn't seem to care that I'd left them. I swung myself up into the saddle, put spur to flank, and whipped the animal mercilessly with the butt of the Henry rifle in my hands. I spurred that horse at a gallop out of the swamp—hazards be damned—then found my way back to the nearest road and high-tailed it north. After an hour or so, I stopped to look over my shoulder, sure that I'd see that shadowy demon from the glade standing just behind me.

"But there was no one. There was only myself, my stolen horse, and our entangled shadows in the moonlight. I spurred him on and the foaming beast carried me. I constantly changed my course, taking long digressions down side roads and along deer and hunting paths. Sometimes I forced the animal to take me straight overland, through thickets and woods and bogs, over untrod fields and pastures. I rode for days... finally for more than a week... until at last I had this town in sight, and knew that I could lay my burden down. Here, I could confess. Here, I could die absolved—and someone would know what we'd done down there in Big Cypress. Someone would know, and they could stop it. With enough guns, enough men—you could stop it."

A fit of coughing wracked him. His whole body seemed to fall into a seizure. He gasped for breath like a man drowning.

"Now, see here," I said, pinning the man with the steeliest gaze I could muster, "I won't have you dying on me, absolved or not."

"But there's nothing left of me," the man said, showing me his bony arms, his filthy hands with their mud-caked nails, the rags of his robes and sweat-saturated clothes beneath. "I'm paper! I'm straw! Hang me up to scare the crows!"

"Damn you, I said no!" I countered, hoping that, like most men, he could be persuaded to hang on to life if only he thought I'd punish him for not doing so. "You were a soldier once, and I say you're a soldier still. I'm an officer, soldier, and I order you to hang on to what life is left in you! Hold on, because we're going to nurse you back to good health, and then we'll all go back there to—"

"No!" he shouted. "No no no no no no no! I won't go back there! You can't make me, ever! I tell you, there's no power on this earth that could drag me back to that benighted swamp!"

He was bucking hard now, and it took half a dozen strong hands to hold him in place. Still he fought against us. I called for a doctor and someone said the man had been sent for, long ago, but Mr. Yates, though allegedly in his death throes, still fought like a lion.

"I won't go!" he shouted.

"You must!" I told him.

Then he surprised us all. In the mad clamor of many warm bodies all pressing forward to hold the struggling man, none of us realized how near Sergeant Mulvaney's sidearm was to Yates's grasp. While we struggled just to hold him still, Yates managed to dive his hand into Mulvaney's holster, yank out his Colt Navy Revolver, and cock its hammer.

We all shrank from the pistol in the Rebel's hand.

Yates put the barrel in his mouth and pulled the trigger.

I would be lying if I said that we spent any great deal of time mourning poor, mad Mr. Yates, or that we were, at that point, much affected by his story. It was true, his sudden appearance, his distemper, and his tale were all strange and most unexpected, but ultimately, it was the drudge of cleaning up after him and the unanswered questions left in the wake of his suicide that upset myself and the men. After all, the men had to sleep in those barracks. How easily would they sleep that night, even after the blood and brain matter had been scoured from the wall?

But, we were soldiers and we had duties to perform. Sergeant Mulvaney assigned two men to clean up and another to find an undertaker to see Yates's body properly boxed and interred. In the meantime, the late Mr. Yates would repose in the tool shed out back, wrapped in the very sheets he had died upon.

The doctor, summoned before Yates's tale ever began, was only located after some hours of searching him out, and arrived with the corporal sent to find him not too long after that fatal bullet had plowed its way through Yates's brain.

"What's happened?" the doctor asked. "Has the poor man already expired?"

"In a manner of speaking," I told him, then excused myself. Yates's tale had taken hours to relate. It was nigh midnight now, and it had been too long since my last drink. Thus, I returned to my favorite saloon, splurged on a bottle of cheap brandy (for even cheap brandy was expensive in that little burg), then lit myself a fresh cigar.

My new friend, the magic lantern peddler, joined me. I asked him how his show had gone and he flashed his wolfish grin and assured me it had gone quite well. I asked him if he sold any of his wares as the result of his picture show. He shook his head and picked lint from the lapel of his crimson coat.

"My sincerest apologies," I said. "It can't be an easy business."

He shrugged a little. "It's not about sales," he said with a strange sort of assurance. "No sir. I trundle my wares from town to town and mount my picture shows for the deeper, surer reward of transmogrifying hearts and minds. So long as just one viewer comes away transformed, well, then—my task is complete, my conscience satisfied."

I thought of the images he had shared with us in that very saloon. The bodies broken by shrapnel on sunlit fields… the tribunal hangings… the dead men in ditches…

"Yours is a holy endeavor, indeed," I said, then called for another glass so that I could share my brandy. The bartender obliged. I poured the fellow a finger or two.

"Much obliged, lieutenant," he said as he drank it down. I swallowed another draught of my own, then refilled my glass.

"Something weighs on you," he said after a time.

I nodded. "I heard a strange story this evening," I said, "punctuated by a suicide."

The peddler seemed troubled at that. "Hells bells," he muttered. "How rude of a man to make his quietus a public spectacle. What, may I ask, was the gist of this story?"

I considered relating it all back to him—he was eager and interested, after all, and I certainly felt compelled to unburden myself—but then, I thought better of it. This poor fellow had no desire to hear the ravings of the late, lunatic Mr. Yates, and I had no true desire to revisit them. Not when I knew damned well I would be required to act upon them.

"Let me ask you a question," I said then. "And I urge you to respond with all candor. In your opinion, just what is it that myself and my kind—soldiers, men in uniform—are doing here, now that the war's done? What purpose do we serve?"

The peddler smiled delightedly, as though his opinion were his most readily offered commodity. He leaned closer, offering his answer in a conspiratorial whisper. "The war is done, indeed," he said, "but you know as well I that the lesson is still not learned."

I nodded. I knew it well. These southerners were a stubborn and unrepentant lot. Even losing the war hadn't convinced them that they were wrong.

"Trample out your vintage where the grapes of wrath are stored, lieutenant" the peddler said encouragingly, his grin as salacious as ever. "Loose the fateful lightning of your terrible, swift sword."

I thanked him—for he had told me precisely what I needed to hear—then made my farewells. I meandered back to my boarding house, eager to put myself to bed. I had drunk enough that I should have been asleep quickly, but it wasn't to be. I lay awake for some time, window wide, febrile air surrounding me. Yates's tale of terror and bloodshed, coming close on the heels of that morbid picture show, had stirred something within me. When I closed my eyes, I saw the killing fields beside Stones River again... heard the pounding of the guns and smelled the stench of spent powder and blood on the grass... saw the ruined faces and splintered bones and blasted husks of my brothers in arms and the Rebs we slaughtered.

Damn Yates. Damn the willpower that made it possible for him to reach us, even so dehydrated and starved as he was. Damn his insistence on tale-telling and absolution before making his final exit to a peaceful oblivion. Damn his whole, degenerate culture, with their pride and their plantations and their assurances of superiority.

Damn them all, for if they could only accept their defeat like men, I and my men could finally go home, finally stop fighting a war that everyone said was already over, but which no one seemed ready to put behind them.

3

I discussed marching the whole detachment down to Calusa County with Sergeant Mulvaney, but we both finally decided that it would be best to see what could be first gleaned with a lighter unit, then send for reinforcements if necessary. We had a local magistrate write warrants of arrest for Orion Bell, Lyle Beresford and George Carver—the only men whose names had been mentioned in the course of Yates's tale—then gathered the necessary provisions. The party would consist of myself, Sergeant Mulvaney, the town marshal—who would act as our guide, knowing the lay of the land—a corporal, and three privates (including the ever-eager Private Cabott), all of whom were chosen because they proclaimed themselves good horsemen, and not afraid of up-close and personal fighting. Finally, with our horses tacked, our saddle bags fat and our powder stores topped, we mounted up and set out. It was an afternoon in early October. The heat and humidity—appearing to abate in the weeks prior—had suddenly, unseasonably, returned.

A barge bore us across Tampa Bay and we disembarked on a sandy shore some twenty miles further south. The boatman said this stretch was referred to as Palma Sola, and consisted of little more than a few anchorite crackers and Spanish fishermen whose huts lined the shores of both the bay and the Calusa River, farther south. We thanked him for the information, off-loaded our horses, and carried on along a ragged, barely-discernable trail into the mosquito-infested palmetto scrub that lay before us.

Late in the day, we reached the Calusa River and crossed by ferry. From the crossing, it was a short ride into Orphea, a settlement (if such could be believed) even more quaggy and mephitic than Tampa. Here was a trade post with even lower aspirations than its unfortunate neighbor to the north, a tight collection of stores, a stable, a hotel and a dry goods supplier, all bordered by broad, dusty streets strewn with horse apples and hosting a populace as parochial and plodding as Tampa's was embittered and indolent. As we rode into town toward the lone hotel (ambitiously dubbed the Royale), I saw a knot of children in a vacant lot, all encircling some unseen wonder that held them rapt. Only when we passed close to them did I see the object of their amusement: two tomcats, their tails tied together by twine, hissing and spinning and scratching at one another in a bloody minuet that could only end with one or the other dead.

As we passed, one of the children—a little mouse-haired girl in a gingham dress—turned to study us. She had the same slack-jawed, bucolic look about her that most of the milling locals in the streets did, but there was something else in her gaze as well—a sort of dull belligerence, a hostility—that chilled the considerable sweat on my back and made me wonder for a moment if this was where we should bed for the night. Scanning the street for other signs of animus did little to assuage my growing suspicion that we would find no warm welcome thereabouts. A number of men and women shuffled along like sleepwalkers in the dusty streets, no doubt undertaking the most banal of errands. But whenever my eyes met the gazes of those somnolent natives, I noted not dismissive indifference or even uneasy curiosity but a very pointed, obtrusive repugnance—a sense that we were intruders of the most unwanted and undesirable sort. Their silent rancor and the insistent—almost maddening—buzzing of cicadas in the late afternoon heat filled me with a creeping dread that words can barely do justice to. I considered giving voice to my misgivings, but the sun was already stretching our shadows and night would soon be upon us. Surely, I thought, there could be nothing for us—duly appointed representatives of the government of the United States, all veterans of combat—to fear from such a tribe of rubes.

The next twelve hours would prove me dangerously mistaken.

We surrendered our horses to a whiskered, foul-mouthed stabler at the livery, then marched as a party, saddle-bags over our shoulders, into the Royale. We found no one in the lobby and stood for a good long while waiting. Outside, the sun fell and the world reddened. The lobby of the Royale was close and airless, and we sweated almost as much while we stood there waiting as we had on our ride from Palma Sola.

A clerk finally appeared, a small, thin fellow with a wrinkled, jowly face and lank, oily hair. He moved with the same, slow, somnolent shuffle as the townsfolk in the street, and he offered no apologies for our wait when he finally showed himself. He simply asked us how many rooms we would like, and if we'd be dining in the Royale that evening.

"Is there anywhere else to dine?" I asked, trying to decide just what it was in his gaze that unnerved me—for this time, it was not naked hatred but something else.

"No, sir," the wall-eyed clerk said.

"Then we'll be dining here," I answered.

His mouth grinned, displaying two rows of yellow-grey teeth like little tombstones. His eyes remained just as blank and vacant as a pair of lightless storefront windows. "Course you will," he said.

And then I knew what it was about him that so unnerved me: for all the moments that we stood there, conversing about rooms and signing the guest register, the little man never once blinked. Not once.

Still, I said nothing.

Our rooms were split between floors—two on the second, two on the third, which was also the top floor. The marshal took the room across the hall, while Mulvaney bunked with the corporal on the second floor, and the two privates shared the room opposite them. Dinner, we were informed, would be served in one hour, so we had time to clean up and prepare ourselves before dining. Since there was no water in the room, and none forthcoming from the lackadaisical clerk, I was at a loss as to just how we were supposed to clean up or prepare ourselves for anything.

I found my own room on that top floor stifling and close, and opened the single window in the hopes of getting some air. For a moment I stood at that window and stared down into the darkening street, intent on soaking up more of the local color. I saw two children and a trio of grown men on the far side of the street staring directly up at my window. They ogled the way carnival patrons might at some rare freak in a steel cage. In the end, I simply surrendered to my weariness and collapsed on the mildew-smelling bed with my boots off. I waited for a sea breeze to come rolling through my window and cool me in the gathering twilight. None came.

Dinner was pleasant enough, even though it unfolded in a morose and muggy darkness thick with gnats and mosquitoes. We ate greens and grits, fresh fish from the sea and fried fowl from the yard, then ended our repast with sweet corn fritters and a bottle of rum (good whiskey was scarce in post-war Florida, but cheap rum was plentiful). The marshal and the two privates struck up a game of blackjack while the rest of us tried to take some evening air on the front porch. Ultimately, though, there were too many mosquitoes and they were very thirsty, so, I pardoned myself and decided to simply retire for the night. Although Sergeant Mulvaney and the corporal lingered, they suggested they would, most likely, soon do the same.

Thus I climbed the many flights of stairs to my attic room, heaved off my boots and peeled away my officer's coat, then laid myself down on the too-soft bed, hot, uncomfortable, still mostly-dressed, but too tired to care. A little breeze stirred through my open window, but it was not enough to comfort me. Nonetheless, I was soon asleep. The day had taken its toll and I was too exhausted to fight slumber any longer.

I woke to the distant but distinct sough of many boots on dry earth. Upon opening my eyes, I found the world around me dark as Erebus. Still, though in a deep darkness I could hear that remote, insistent sound—like a number of men shuffling along a dirt road in close array. Having traveled many hundreds of miles with military columns, it was certainly a sound I was accustomed to. I had no ken of what time it might be, but it felt as if some hours had elapsed since I fell to sleep. Slowly, carefully, I swung my stockinged feet off the bed, rose, and moved across the bare wooden floor toward the open window.

The streets below were dimly lit, for all the lights in all the stores and houses up and down Orphea's main street were doused. There was only wan moon and starlight, the moon nothing more than a thin, nail-like sliver in the sky. Nonetheless, in that manifold darkness I thought I saw a number of covert figures moving along the street that fronted the hotel, each in turn disappearing beyond my narrow field of vision. I could not say how many there were, or what their ultimate destination was, but it seemed that the sound of their passage—the sound that had awakened me—suggested numbers, and their movement suggested they might be gathering before or even inside the hotel.

A light knock came at my door. I nearly jumped out of my socks. For a tense and pregnant moment I stood there by the window, loath to speak, unable to move, wondering just who might be approaching my room at such an hour, rapping so furtively.

Then, a voice. It was Private Cabott, hissing through the door, little more than a stage whisper. He was calling my name.

I crossed immediately to the door and threw it open. The young man stood there in the darkened hall, the frightened look on his pale face barely discernible in the gloom.

"What's the trouble, private?" I asked in a whisper of my own, the silence all around us seeming too precious—too protective—to violate with even conversational voices.

"Lieutenant," the young man said, "there are people downstairs. We think they're getting ready to come up the stairs."

"Come up the stairs for what?" I asked, though I already had my suspicions.

"For us, sir," the private said.

Before I could ask what made him think that, I heard a creaking on the stairs off to our right and stepped out of the door of my room to see just what was coming for us. It turned out to be the other private, the corporal, and Sergeant Mulvaney. They had their saddle-bags and gear in motley disarray in their hands and on their shoulders: clearly, they were ready to bid the Royale a hasty midnight adieu.

"We were right," Mulvaney whispered. "They're gathering."

"Wake the marshal," I said, without a moment's hesitation. "I'll get my things."

While they did as instructed, I snatched up and drew on my boots, then saw to the rest of my accouterments. I had, luckily, not unpacked much, so it took me less than a minute to shrug on my blue coat, strap shut my saddlebags, and throw them over my shoulder. By the time I emerged into the hallway, bearing with me a lit hurricane lamp, the wick trimmed low, the marshal had appeared, similarly outfitted, and the six of us were ready to go.

But where could we go? We were on the third floor of the hotel, with our only likely means of egress being either the stairs—which were blocked on the ground floor by the midnight party that had come for us—or one of several small windows, all opening onto the pitched roof or the hotel's sheer east and west walls.

Below, we heard boots shuffling back and forth across the creaking floorboards of the lobby. There was movement, but not a hint of voices or conversation. It was as though everything that transpired down there transpired in absolute silence. For some reason, that fact unsettled me.

Then, we heard it: the groan of the lowest stair as the first boots mounted and climbed. Their ascent was slow and insistent, but it sounded like there were a great many of them—too many to take stock of in the darkness, separated by two floors.

It was Sergeant Mulvaney's idea to leap from the roof of the Royale to the adjacent roof of the livery stable. True, this would require venturing out onto the pitched roof of the hotel itself, crawling on our bellies to its nearest corner, making an astounding leap across twenty feet of empty space, then falling just as far onto the livery's roof, but we had no other means of escaping the hotel. At best, we could slip into the stable, snatch our horses, and ride swiftly out of this very unwelcoming little town. At worst, we might take shelter somewhere below that presented better options for both defense and withdrawal than the blasted third floor of this little hotel.

Either way, our options were few.

To show that it could be done, Sergeant Mulvaney went first. The posse below could already be heard rising toward us, almost to the landing on the second floor, an unending parade of heavy bodies and quietly-stepping boots. Still, there was no voice apparent, not a word uttered. I had never met the raiding party that could execute its duty in absolute silence. I turned to the marshal.

"What do you think?" I asked. "Do we challenge them? Try to negotiate?"

The marshal's eyes were wide and fearful. He didn't strike me as a callow or cowardly man—quite the opposite in fact— but at that moment, he was clearly affrighted by whatever plans he imagined our midnight visitors to have in store for us. I hoped that he understood what I was really asking him. These are your folk, I wanted to say, your neighbors, after a fashion. Do we open fire? Can you, being local, live with that? Try as I might, though, I couldn't put it so baldly.

He understood, though, for he finally shuddered the slightest and shook his head. "I don't think this bodes well," he said. "So many men, coming for us in the middle of the night… I don't know that they'd be open to negotiation."

I looked to the window. Private Cabott was on his way out.

"Then we'd better slow them down," I said. "Go back into your room and bring me the lamp."

While he did as I asked, I moved nearer to the stair rail. I didn't peer over the side, down the stairwell, but I listened. Below, I heard the boots tromping up toward our landing. I heard so many feet on those quietly creaking stairs that I imagined an unbroken line of men—single-file, like ants—stretching all the way back down to the ground floor.

The second private slid out the window. As he edged out onto the shingles, the marshal emerged from his room and handed me his lamp. I set down my own lamp—still burning—and removed the glass chimney from the marshal's own. I then snatched up my own lamp again and used its burning wick to light the marshal's. It was time to tip our hand and let them know that they hadn't caught us in our beds after all.

"We can hear you," I called down the stairwell, "and we know there are a lot of you! I demand to know what the meaning of this intrusion is!"

No answer came. I heard only breathing and the creaking of the stairs as boots shuffled in place. I wished desperately that our attackers would just announce their intentions, however hostile. Their silence was far more frightening than any threat would be.

"Withdraw!" I shouted, "I am an officer of the Army of these United States and neither I nor my men will stand for being threatened!"

Still no reply. I glanced over my shoulder. The corporal—the last save for the marshal and myself—was just disappearing out the window.

No more warnings. I stepped forward and hurled one of the lamps down the stairwell. It hit the landing below us, shattered, and the lamp oil came alight, a ghostly scintillation of blue and orange flame that lit the entire stairwell. In the light from the conflagration, I saw a number of faces, all staring up at me. They wore masks made of flower sacks and pillow cases, and there were weapons in their hands, from rifles and pistols to pitchforks and axes. Most shrank from the flames. One fellow took aim with a pistol and fired. I withdrew away from the top landing just as his pistol shot sheared splinters off the railing.

"Go!" I told the marshal.

He seemed puzzled for a moment, until I jerked my head toward the window. Finally he understood. As he hurried to the window and went shimmying out, I stepped up to the stair rail again and hurled his lamp down. It burst on the landing of the floor below, about six feet from where the first puddle of lamp oil was now burning. The two pools of flame coalesced into a great conflagration, licking at the dusty throw rugs and the peeling wallpaper. The men in the sack masks pressed forward, snatching up any carpet or runner they could to try and beat out the flames.

I retreated to the window. Before climbing through I took a look. Out along the pitched roof of the hotel, I saw the corporal and the marshal, both making their way on their bellies along the shingles toward the corner nearest the stable roof far below. Down on the stable roof, I could see two more bodies in the wan starlight, though in that dimness, I could not tell who it was.

Then, like a fool, I looked down. Over the edge of the roof, past the rusty rain-gutters, it was a thirty or forty foot drop.

That doesn't sound like much, perhaps, but when it's a span of empty space between you and the solid ground, I promise you it seems far more frightening. Worse, I could see something dark and huddled down on the dusty alley floor between the hotel and the stable. Although there was little light to see by, I could just make out the outline of one boot, and a single splayed-open hand.

Someone—I could not tell who—had fallen in their attempt to traverse the roof. They weren't moving.

Still, I couldn't linger. I wriggled out through the window and did my best to block out the sound of boots tromping up from below. Any moment, the local vigilance committee would be leaping through those dying flames and come pounding up those stairs. Desperate not to fall and end up a broken heap on the ground below, I threw my body flat against the slant of the roof and started scooting, face down, toward the far corner.

The corporal and the marshal made their leaps, one after the other. I couldn't see—my face was pressed against the shingles—but I heard each of them thump against the stable roof in turn and grunt, expelling air as they made contact. I was nearly to the corner of the roof and ready to take my own plunge when I saw a head in a sack mask appear out of the very window I had made my escape from. Without thinking, my hand fell to the holster at my side. It was awkward, but I managed to draw my weapon, take aim, and cock back the hammer. The pistol I carried was a family heirloom—a big, ponderous Walker Colt given me by my father, a veteran of the Mexican War. It weighed five pounds fully loaded and fired a forty-four caliber lead ball. Though my hand shook, I squeezed the trigger. That Walker roared and a great swatch of wood sheared away from the window frame in a shower of sawdust and splinters. The man who had dared to peer out disappeared back into the window like a tortoise retreating into his shell. I fired twice more—hoping to dissuade any more curious followers, then holstered my pistol and rolled my head to get a better vantage of the leap I was about to make.

I saw the others on the roof of the stable, slowly crawling in through the hay loft doors on the upper floor. I had no more time to spare, and every moment that passed was another moment for our would-be murderers to run back downstairs and surround us in the stable before we could make our escape. Without thinking, I rolled my body over so that I was on my back instead of my stomach, rose up onto my feet, then took a lunging leap off the hotel roof and went falling through space.

It seemed to take forever. For just a moment, I thought I had miscalculated, that I'd miss the roof entirely and keep falling to the dusty earth below. But no—I was lucky. I hit the livery stable roof, felt the wind knocked out of me, then started tumbling downward along its rake. Before I went barreling over the lip of the stable roof, I saw shadows at the open hay loft door. They were reaching out for me. I reached out for them, and just as I fell into space once more, two strong hands locked onto my right hand and wrist. They let me swing to arrest my motion, then hauled me up into the hayloft.

It was Sergeant Mulvaney and the corporal.

"Gentlemen," I managed, breathing so heavily I thought I might choke, "I owe each of you a bottle of good whiskey when this is all over."

"Just maintaining the chain of command," Mulvaney quipped. "Let's be on our way now, sir."

I agreed. Below, the marshal and Private Cabott already had the horses out of their stalls, ready to ride.

We made it, but just barely. By the time we had all mounted and were whipping our horses out through the open door of the stable, the masked men that had come to do us harm were pouring out of the Hotel Royale into the streets. Above us, flames and smoke poured from some upper windows, indicating that their efforts to douse the fire were all for naught.

Still, they didn't seem to care about that at the moment. As we came galloping out of the livery yard and into the street, they swarmed toward us, raising their weapons and letting loose a barrage of buckshot and ball that, miraculously, didn't touch a one of us. I couldn't count them all, but there were quite a few—somewhere between twenty and fifty.

All for us.

My God, is that every man in the city limits? I remember thinking. *Are we so despised, so dangerous, that so many could be persuaded to join the lynching party and abet our executions?*

I shoved the thought from my mind as a ball whizzed by my left ear. Heart pounding and blood thumping like a drum at my temples, I bent forward over my mount's withers, dug in my heels, and whipped her rump with my reins. We all went galloping out of town at breakneck speed, following the road for a mile or two before finally slowing to regroup. Once we were all together again, I was reminded that our party was one man down.

It had been the other private that I'd seen lying in the alleyway far below me when I ventured onto the roof. He hadn't made it. And worse—I'd left his dead and broken body back in that shoddy little town to suffer whatever depredations those secessionist devils could provide it. Realizing this, I was ashamed of myself.

But I was alive and so were the others.

Better, no one seemed to be following us.

Satisfied, we carried on at a more reasonable pace, riding all night until the first purple light of day came creeping over the palms and pines and the morning birds began to sing. By that time, we were all exhausted, but silently exultant for our state of being.

We were alive. Gloriously alive.

For that moment, it was enough.

At dawn, we made camp in a fenced but unmowed field just a stone's throw from the road, underneath the shade of a great old live oak. No one wanted to talk about what had transpired—we only wanted sleep. I took the first watch and everyone bedded down on the bare ground. After two hours I woke Sergeant Mulvaney, who took the second watch, and I let sleep take me. There were no dreams, no portents. It felt as though I had barely closed my eyes, barely surrendered to my exhaustion and weariness, when someone was gently shaking me, begging me to open them again. In the seemingly-instant interval between closing my eyes and opening them, several hours had passed.

Awake and somewhat refreshed, we prepared a hasty meal with some of the provisions in our saddlebags. It was only then—a pot of coffee boiling over an open fire, some rations in our bellies—that we found the wherewithal to discuss what had almost become of us the night before. It was shortly after noon. The sun high and the cicadas trilled belligerently in the mid-day heat. The shade beneath the oak was considerable, but hardly cool.

"Let this be a reminder," I told the men sternly, "that we're in hostile territory." I said this as much for my own benefit as for theirs. "While we may not run into another band of murderous thugs in masks, we can't count on any help or cooperation."

"Forgive me, sir," Private Cabott said, "but shouldn't we then go back to Tampa and return with the whole troop? Isn't that the only way to be sure we won't be taken by surprise again?"

"Keep your opinions to yourself," Mulvaney growled. "That's your commanding officer you're speaking to, private!"

"No," I said, "he's got a point. Perhaps we should go back. I'm open to discussing it."

No one spoke for a long interval. It was the marshal who finally chimed in.

"Well, sir," said he, "I can lead us back to the city by another route that would take us far afield of Orphea. It would also add several days to our journey, because we'd be going the long way around the bay. I know you've lost a man and that none of us expected what happened last night, but we're here now. From where I sit, the only sensible thing is to carry on to Bellhaven, try to lay hands on the three men we've got warrants for, and only then retreat to Tampa."

"But what if we're not so lucky next time?" the corporal asked. "We've still got to eat and sleep. We can't get by down here for long, always looking over our shoulders, terrified of who might come for us in the night."

"These are farmers and field hands," Mulvaney growled. "We are soldiers. We don't retreat for a bunch of obstreperous grey-backs who think they can go on defying the will of the United States government!"

"I'm inclined to agree with you, sergeant, sir," the corporal countered, "but just in case you haven't noticed, we're outnumbered hereabouts."

Mulvaney's scowl made it clear that he didn't like hearing arguments from his subordinates. Try as I might, I couldn't summon the same sense of insult or affront. For one thing, the corporal was right. We were outnumbered. In addition, at that moment I felt like the most loutish and incompetent commander that the uniform had ever been hung upon. Why I ever thought that we could ride away from the bulk of our troop and the relative safety of the city for a hostile, backward countryside full of embittered seceshes was beyond me. Had I honestly not anticipated any sort of resistance? Any sort of mischief or subterfuge? I had fatally underestimated the fury of the hornet's nest we had collectively kicked, and it had already cost us one man's life.

Would I add insult to injury now, and insist that we carry on?

But what else could we do? As the marshal said, our safest route home would take us days out of our way. To beat such a slow retreat with nothing to show for it, and barely a day after we'd set out—it seemed just as wrong as the perhaps misplaced hubris that told me to go on.

"I move we put it to a vote," the corporal said tentatively.

"We'll do no such bloody thing!" Mulvaney snapped. "This is still a military unit on a military mission, corporal, and as such it's under the command of just one person, and that's the ranking officer! At the moment, Lieutenant Kenning remains your lawful commander, and we'll do only what he commands us to do! Is that understood?"

The corporal looked duly chastised. I felt sorry for him. Before Sergeant Mulvaney had so summarily dressed the man down, I was ready to do just as the corporal suggested—to put the matter to a vote. I hadn't drilled the men for months. Military discipline was a thing of the past, and everyone knew it. Why, then, should we carry on the charade at such a moment? Their lives were on the line, just as mine was. If we were in equal danger, shouldn't we share the burden of deciding whether to ride toward it or flee from it?

But then I heard a voice in my head offer an answer. *They need you*, it said. *They need their commanding officer to command, to give them courage, and to assure them everything will be all right in the end.*

If need be, they need you to lie to them.

And to yourself.

I was damned, no matter which way I turned.

"The marshal's right," I said. "There's no way out of this mess but straight through it. To turn back now would dishonor that poor boy's sacrifice and make the rest of us look like cowards. The only way we're going home is with at least one of those three men that we came looking for—and we'll only settle for one if a thorough search for the other two proves fruitless. Is that understood?"

Yes, sir, they all said, even the marshal.

I cursed myself for a coward and a fool, then drank my coffee.

Within the hour we pressed on, agreeing that we should not tempt fate—and our would-be captors—any longer by lingering in that weedy field. By two in the afternoon, our saddlebags were once more laden, our horses well-rested, and we were on our way. The trilling, maddening song of the cicadas showed no signs of abating. I started to think the damned things were following us, making their hellish, buzzing racket so that the people of Orphea could eventually hunt us down.

Bellhaven, the marshal told us, was about fifteen miles south-southeast of our present position. We traveled the rest of the day along a broad, well-beaten thoroughfare known locally as Wingate Road, and finally turned eastward at a crossroads emptying onto a less well-kept path that sported wheel-ruts and the marks of passage, but that was also overgrown and weedy in such a way as to suggest the people didn't much pass that way any longer. By late afternoon, when the sun fell toward the treetops, we still had not reached our destination. Being quite parched and seeing no readily apparent sign of a spring or stream, we decided to dare a visit to a local homestead.

There was a plank farmhouse set far back from the path very near to the crossroads where we would turn east toward Bellhaven. Seeing even from a distance that the house boasted a well and a horse trough, we nosed our horses up the dirt lane that led to it and made our approach. After a time, I started to wonder if any one even lived in the shoddy little cottage, because no one came to greet us and no shadows moved in its glass-less front windows. But, as we emerged from the tree-lined lane into the late gathering twilight, we suddenly saw the door to the little cabin swing open. A man stepped out. From a distance, he looked thoroughly ordinary—of average height and build, with sandy hair and a trimmed beard and everyday work clothes covered in dust and no doubt redolent of sweat and tilled earth. I raised my hand in greeting. The man of the house offered none in return.

Closer, and I could finally see him clearly. He stood there before his open door, staring at us, still as a statue, hands hanging at his sides placidly. In the shadows beyond the door, I thought I saw a flash of calico and a pale, moony face, but the figure that the swatch of color and the face belonged to slipped back into the shadows before I could be sure. I assumed that was the lady of the house, content to let her husband greet the newcomers.

I rode to within thirty feet of the fellow and stopped. "Good afternoon, sir," I said, in as friendly a manner as I could manage.

I waited for a reply and got none. The fellow just stood staring at me, like there was some addendum to the greeting that I should offer, yet had not. I decided to press on. I didn't care for the way he stared at me.

Without blinking.

Just like the clerk at the Royale.

"Are you the owner of this homestead?" I asked.

He gave a slight nod and grunt. His eyes never left me.

"Well, sir, my men and I are on a routine patrol of the area, and our water stores are dangerously low. I wondered if perhaps we could refill our canteens from your well and let our horses drink from your trough?"

The farmer stared. I waited for him to blink, to lower his eyes, to study my men as they hove up behind me. He did nothing of the sort. His gaze remained fixed and unwavering on me.

Suddenly, he spoke. "Go on," he said. "You're welcome." The words were friendly enough, but they seemed out of place coming out of that staring, impassive face—a friendly accommodation from a ventriloquist's dummy.

There was something else as well. I couldn't lay a name to it at that moment, but as I stood there staring at the fellow, I was sure that there was something off about him—something thoroughly, yet subtly, unnatural. I tried to give name to it, but could not. His gaze was a constant distraction and made the notice of any more subtle peculiarities in his manner or his appearance more difficult to tease out.

Best to get on with it, then, I thought, and dismounted. I thanked our host and urged the men to get on with their business. For the next fifteen minutes, myself, the sergeant and the corporal all took turns refilling the party's canteens at the well, while Private Cabott and the marshal saw to watering the horses at the trough. During our sabbatical, I kept stealing glances at our host, trying to put my finger on just what was wrong about him, aside from that glassy, bedazzled stare of his. I also tried to get a look at his missus inside the cabin, through the open door. I failed on both counts. My mind was too encumbered with fear and misgiving to concentrate on the problem that was the farmer, and the gloom beyond the front door of his house was far too deep to penetrate from outside.

Finally, we were done. Each of our canteens was full to the brim, and we and our horses had all had long, satisfying drinks of the vaguely sulfuric water in the farmer's well. In an effort to show the utmost courtesy, I crossed the yard to our puzzling host. I removed my riding glove as I went and offered my hand in thanks.

"Much obliged," I said, and honestly, I meant it. Unsettling stare or no, the fellow had saved us by letting us drink from his well. We were in his debt.

He finally lowered his eyes, this time to stare at the hand I had offered. He stared for a long, awkward moment, then reached out and took it. We shook. When I felt his hand in mine, I knew what it was about him that was bothering me.

His skin did not seem supple, as flesh should. Nor was it rough and leathery, as one might expect a farmer's hands to be. No, the fellow's palm felt hard and dry in my hand, and vaguely fibrous. It was as though his skin had hardened, and was now more chitinous than fleshy. Shaking hands with him was not like shaking hands with a man at all—it was like holding a fat, hard-shelled grasshopper in my hand, and I didn't care for that feeling one bit. That, I realized, was what had been troubling me about the man all along: even though distance and the twilight hid it somewhat, my eyes could still detect the strangeness of his hard, fibrous skin—the very wrongness of it.

Still, I tried not to give my disgust away. I willed the smile on my lips to stay right where it was and I looked that strange man with the chitinous skin right in the eye.

"We owe you a debt," I said, still trying to express my thanks.

"And we'll see it paid," the man whispered, his voice barely audible, the words spoken from between stiff, unmoving lips.

I withdrew my hand, returned to my horse and mounted up. We rode out of the yard and I never once dared to look back.

We camped in another long-unattended field about a half mile up the road. If anyone owned that field or took umbrage with our utilizing it, they did not show themselves to say so. Once more, we broke out our supplies from the saddlebags, a fire was made, and an evening meal undertaken. I said nothing to the others about the strangeness I noted in our host at the farm. Nonetheless, I seemed to feel all their eyes upon me, as if they, too, suspected something and awaited my report.

Stubbornly, I kept the matter to myself. Eventually, someone asked how far we were from our destination, and I knew that no one would press me on the matter of what I knew that I would not speak of.

"We should reach the Bellhaven neighborhood tomorrow," the marshal assured us.

"I shall be tickled pink," I muttered sardonically, and bade Sergeant Mulvaney spike my coffee with some whiskey from his flask.

"Sir," Cabott asked me as the fire crackled and the numberless stars all crawled up the dark firmament behind the last, wan light of day, "do you think any of it's true?"

I studied the young man. While his question seemed casual enough, I could see by the firm set of his lips and the knit in his brow that he was troubled. Clearly, Yates's story about Orion Bell and his blasphemous books and his accords with ancient gods had burrowed into the boy and now worked on his natural superstitious inclinations.

"Some of it's probably true," I said. "Cowards in masks tearing through the countryside stirring up the negroes and stringing them from trees—that's probably true. You read the papers. You know all about the upsets in Tennessee and the Carolinas."

"But the rest of it," Cabott said.

"Hogwash," Mulvaney said with a huff, and spat into the fire.

I couldn't answer so quickly, or so confidently. My natural skepticism warred with the primitive part of me that believed in all sorts of strange and horrifying and miraculous things. I wanted to tell Cabott that it was, as Sergeant Mulvaney said, all hogwash. Part of me certainly felt that way. Truth be told, with every battle I survived and every body I saw ruined by violence—and the numbers of bodies I'd seen so ruined were many—I had found it increasingly difficult to believe in anything beyond the material. I was raised a good Methodist, and I'd marched to war with prayers on my lips and hymns in my heart. But on that muggy autumn eve in that weedy Floridian field, with the war just a few years behind me and all those awful memories so near and so vivid… well, let's just say I had come to accept that there either was no god at all, or that any god or gods that might exist beyond the pale of the every day were as indifferent to our plights and sufferings as men were to the passions of ants, or the prayers of horseflies. Believing so, how could I put much credence in the late Mr. Yates's fantastic tales of arcane tomes full of potent magic and rites that conjured eight foot tall men of shadow out of thin air? It was madness, all of it—the rambling inventions of a guilt-ridden, fevered mind.

And yet… and yet…

"It's these swamps," the marshal told the private, smiling as a father might when assuring his child that the thunder held no threat, only empty clamor. "I don't know what it's like where you're from, son, but hereabouts, the night's thick and the air's alive. The shadows in the swamps can move of their own accord. Even the bravest men, the most sensible and unimaginative of men, can start to see phantoms and hear voices and conjure haunts when he's lost among the cypresses, or trudging about under the moss and the pines. Listen now— just listen."

We all listened. Beyond the crackling of the fire, we heard the trilling of katydids, the intermittent scampering of field mice through the high grasses, and the alternating hoots and screeches of owls in barns or far-flung trees. Frogs croaked in throaty chorale, the wind hitched, and the wiregrass whispered for its passage.

The night was, indeed, alive.

"Now," the marshal finally said, after a long and deliberate silence, "just imagine that, but deeper, more insistent. The swamp can be so loud at night, you'd think it was speaking just to you, trying to get your attention. And with all those sounds come shapes and shadows. That Mr. Yates—from what you say, it sounds to me like he was mad with grief, still fighting the war in his own head and heart. He saw ghosts and devils where there was nothing more than men, doing evil, as men are wont to do."

"So there's nothing to be afraid of in the swamp?" Private Cabott asked.

The marshal lowered his eyes, rubbed his hands together slowly. "No, son, I didn't say that."

Cabott didn't say much after that. None of us did.

It was the following day, well after noon, that we arrived in the vicinity of Bellhaven Plantation. I asked the marshal to guide us to some of the local negro settlements, but he apologized and pointed out that, while he knew where to find the plantation, he had no idea where the freedmen's settlements had cropped up since the end of the war. Thus, we rode on along our weedy, dusty track through the sun-dappled wilderness, sweating ourselves skinny and doing battle with the ever-more belligerent clouds of blowflies and mosquitoes that assailed us.

Just around a bend, we came upon a family of negroes trudging along the trail. We saw them clearly, at a distance, just a moment before they noticed us. The moment they saw us, they froze in their tracks. A moment later, they ducked off the road into the thick forest and underbrush.

I immediately nosed my horse around to face the men. I ordered half of them to dismount and venture into the woods, the other half to follow me up the road. We galloped toward the spot where the negroes had quit the trail, to quickly close the distance between their party and ours, then dismounted and trudged into the woods after them.

"Hello there!" I called, doing my best to project my voice but also to sound friendly. "There's no need to be frightened. We're soldiers and we're not hear to hurt anyone."

Off to my right, something rustled in a stand of scrub hickory. I saw two black bodies—small and fleet—break from cover, then disappear once more as they darted away from us through the pines. I followed them, my pace insistent, but not at a dead run. The marshal and Sergeant Mulvaney spread out on either side of me and followed me on more or less the same course.

"Now, see here," I said, again trying to sound as reasonable as I could but afraid that I was still coming across as desperate or belligerent, "we're in this area looking for some fugitives— white fugitives—and we could use your help. Don't keep leading us on such a merry chase!"

There again, farther off to my right, another set of black bodies—three this time, larger and clearly older than the children I'd been following—broke from cover in a thicket of firebush and skittered over the pine-needle strewn forest floor toward some tarflower growing thick beneath a stand of acacia. Further on, about a hundred yards away, I saw the corporal and Private Cabott picking their way through the underbrush, approaching the hidden negroes from the opposite direction. Could we trap them by closing in from both sides? Should we? After all, if they and their folk had been suffering the depredations of Orion Bell and his vigilantes for the last few months, why shouldn't they run from strange white men encountered on the road? When we had gone to war to free them but failed to protect them from their former overseers, why should they trust any of us?

"Listen to me," I said, and the voice that I spoke in was raw, and tired, and quite desperate. It was honest and came from the weary center of me. "We don't want to hurt anyone. We're in danger ourselves. If you could just come out and speak to us for a moment, we could be on our way and you on yours. You have my word that no one will harm you or detain you."

Some palmettos off to my left rustled. I stole a glance toward them and thought I saw white eyes in black faces staring out from the shadows beneath them.

Not twenty feet ahead of me, one of them stepped out of a hickory copse. I couldn't believe that someone had been hiding so close to me and I had not seen them. She was a handsome woman of some forty years, and although her face had a bold and dusky beauty about it, her eyes held murder. I knew that look: it was undiluted rage.

"Hello there," said I, doing my best to seem affable and unthreatening, for truly we meant this group no harm. "I'm Lieutenant Nathan Kenning. What's your name?"

"What do you want?" she asked through gritted teeth.

"We're in search of some white men who we believe to be causing trouble hereabouts. Might you be able to tell us where to find them?"

She smiled a little. It was a bitter, mordant smile that suggested I was in over my head and fumbling toward a precipice. "You should go," she said.

I tried to meet her gaze and reply without hesitation. "We're soldiers, ma'am. We don't scare easily."

"Then you're fools," she said, and I detected no more bitterness in her voice. There was only a sort of resigned sadness now. Her expression softened as well.

The rest of her party began to emerge from their hiding places. There were mostly women and children. The only men were gawky teenagers or wrinkled, toothless oldsters. All of them bore bundles and sacks and baskets for the journey, probably with provisions and whatever material goods they deemed worth transporting. All of them had a look in their eyes that sent a real, physical shudder through me, for it was a look I knew well. I saw it in the mirror more often than not, and knew it instantly when I saw it in the eyes of fellow soldiers.

It was the haunted stare of the walking dead. The eyes of the damned.

What had these people suffered to give them that look?

"Let's cut to the chase, then," I said. "The rumors are true, aren't they? They've raised an army and they ride by night?"

"They've raised hell," she said, "and they'll drag you there if you hunt them."

"Where are you going, then?"

"Away," she said. "If we can."

"We can protect you," I said.

"You can't," she answered, then turned, fixed the others with her stare, and cocked her head back toward the road. She looked to me once more. "We're leaving now."

Sergeant Mulvaney lunged forward. "Now, wait just a minute—"

I held out my hand to silence him. It would do no good. These people weren't just migrants—they were refugees. The war was still being fought in Calusa County.

"I wish you well," I told the woman as she trudged past me, her followers close behind her.

"Turn around," she said. "Go back now."

She didn't wait to see if her words made any impression on me. She simply picked a path back through the underbrush to the road, then turned at the tree line to make sure that all of her followers were accounted for. Once they had all passed her and taken once more to the road, she threw a final look of sad reproach back at me, then turned her back on me and joined her party. They marched on, back the way we had come.

I turned to Sergeant Mulvaney. My voice was barely a whisper, my words only for him. "Did you see their eyes?"

He met my gaze and nodded. Then, at last, I knew the truth: Sergeant Mulvaney was as frightened as I was.

"Do we carry on?" I asked quietly, hoping that the corporal and Private Cabott weren't close enough to hear me.

"We must," Mulvaney answered, then turned back toward the road.

We returned to our horses and carried on.

We rejoined the road and followed it as it turned full south. It was just as the sun kissed the treetops and the shadows of twilight began to swallow that overgrown track in the woods that we came upon a pair of stone pillars and a bronze marker: the proper entrance to storied Bellhaven. We all drew in our reins and sat our horses there for a moment, studying the sign and the pillars, hardly believing that we had finally made our destination.

"Is this it, then?" I asked the marshal.

"Aye, sir," he said. "This is it."

I led the way.

The long drive wound through groves of myrtle, laurel and magnolia, all purpling in the dusk, crowding in upon the path. In the gloaming we passed long-untended orchards and small meadows choked by crabgrass and yellow tickseed. Little by little, without word or signal, we increased our pace, moving from an easy gait into an eager canter, none of us wanting to be caught in those groves once the sun was down. More than once I found myself peering into the gathering gloom at knotty old oaks and the gnarled magnolias, sure that my eyes were playing tricks on me. I seemed to be hallucinating, but only at the periphery of my vision. Every time I turned my eyes forward to follow the path, I was sure I saw those great, dark boughs dip and move, as though reaching out toward us, positive I saw watching eyes and glowering faces pressing out of the boles and knots of the trees to mark our passing with stern disapproval. Nonetheless, despite my misgivings, whenever I dared look into those darkened stands I saw only convocations of lonely trees, mindful but unmoving. Once more I drove my spurs into my horse's flank. She increased her pace.

At long last the groves thinned. The drive emerged from the impenetrable darkness under a pair of arcing, sentinel oaks. There before us, beyond a haggard lawn and copses of hoary bush that were once flower beds, the glowering old manse rose up in the twilight like a pale apparition.

I must say, the place struck me upon my first clear sight of it as a perfect reflection of its tragic history. Once, perhaps, it was a handsome place, its white pillars gleaming, its brick walls rich and red as Georgia clay, its box hedges and flower beds well-tended and all in bloom. Idly imagining its glorious past, I could almost smell the spring magnolias, see the bright azaleas and champion roses below the front windows and hear the rhythmic chants of the slaves in the field. I imagined that once upon a time, before the war, before the world was rent and torn and shattered, this place had been someone's home, and a good one at that.

But no longer. Bellhaven was now a ghost of its former self. Sickly ivy crawled up those pillars on the front porch, the hedges were all overgrown and formless, and the beds of flowers were now just kingdoms for sandbur and dandelion, keeping pace with the wild growth of the unmowed wiregrass on the lawn around them. Every window was lightless, and the live oaks and magnolia trees that grew closest to the house all seemed twisted and misshapen, warped somehow by the sad end of their one-time master or the blasphemous undertakings of their new one.

Bellhaven was no longer a home. It was now a tomb.

I decided at that moment to give it some corpses so that it could feel useful.

There was an old, worn-down hitching post in the yard before the porch. We reined in our horses and dismounted. The moment we were off of them, our animals fussed, stamped and shook their heads. Something had them agitated. At least two of the horses tried to bite their riders and slip their reins, but we all managed to hold onto them and get them tied. Tying them off didn't calm them, though. They continued to stamp and snort and to struggle against their bridles, all five of them affrighted, eager to be away from that darksome, dreadful plantation house.

I didn't blame them. It was only an act of will and the thought of what a fool I would look like before my men that kept me from announcing the expedition a failure, putting myself back in the saddle, and riding the hell out of there. My fear and my determination were at war with one another, and at any given moment, I had little ken of which one was winning.

I ordered Private Cabott to stay with the horses while the rest of us entered the house. Of the men remaining, I sent Sergeant Mulvaney and the corporal round back, while the marshal and I approached via the front door. We waited until

Mulvaney and the private were out of sight, then mounted the long-unswept porch steps.

The house had a ground floor, but its lack of a front entrance and the rise of the porch steps toward the level above told us that the ground floor consisted of little more than servants' quarters, perhaps a visitor's entrance round back and work spaces that needed to be close to the house for the sake of convenience, but separated from the living spaces in the interest of propriety. As we climbed the front steps, the marshal and I each studied the massive, ivy-choked pillars that loomed above and around us. Likewise, the black and empty windows suddenly took on the uncomfortable aspect of deep and ancient eyes peering out at us from a drooping, time-ruined face. I felt it deep within me and involuntarily shuddered. A quick glance told me that the marshal suffered the same feeling. When we stepped onto the broad, high front porch of the old manse, it felt like we were stepping into the portico of some ancient temple in a faraway land, not the threshold of a plantation house in torrid Florida.

We studied the porch. There were old rockers, long bleached by the sun, as well as a number of planters that no doubt once held flowers, but that now sported little more than dry earth and dead, brown flora. I crossed the porch, took hold of the knocker on the front door, and sounded it three times.

We waited. Around us, the color slowly bled out of the world as night gathered and the sun's last light faded. I threw a glance back at Private Cabott. He stood out at the hitching post with the horses, eyes wide and wary in the gloom, shaking hands wrapped around a Henry rifle.

I knocked at the door again. Once more, no answer came.

"Are these gentlemen callers, come to bend my ear and watch the sun go down beside me?"

The voice startled us both. The marshal and I spun away from the front door, instinct turning us toward the greeting. The marshal raised his double-barreled shotgun. My hand fell to the big, heavy Walker Colt on my hip.

The voice—honeyed and melodious, with the unmistakable lilt of the South—belonged to a young woman. She stood far off toward the right wing of the house, having apparently just appeared from the far side. She was small and wiry, and she wore what looked like a filthy, yellowing wedding dress that had clearly seen better days. Her hair was a wild tangle of mousy curls and her eyes bulged madly from a skeletal face. Once, she might have been beautiful, but presently, she looked like the gaunt and pallid waif who haunted the windswept moors of a Gothic romance.

This had to be Livia Bell, the mad sister of the man we sought. If her lunatic gaze and long-degraded wedding dress did not clearly announce her state of mind, the bundles of dying blue clustervine, red lily, and skullcap in her hands and the Tread Softly woven into her hair would have made it amply apparent. She made me think of all the Ophelias in all the productions of Hamlet that I had ever been witness to—but real; terribly, undeniably, pathetically real in a way that no stage lunatic could ever be.

I let my hand drift away from my holster. "Are you the lady of the house?"

She smiled, an expression that looked positively ghoulish in that thin and sickly face. "I am, kind sir, but good manners dictate you announce yourself before I give you formal greeting. It's getting on dark, after all, and I don't usually meet my callers so late."

I stepped forward. "Nathan Kenning," I said, bowing a little to try and feed the woman's delusion and keep her from giving us away too readily. "And I should be most pleased to spend the evening in your company, m'lady."

Livia Bell gave a morbid, coquettish laugh, then approached the steps. Off to our left, at the hitching post, Private Cabott watched the proceedings with confused horror. I signaled for him to sit tight and stay quiet.

Miss Bell had reached the porch now. She stood an arm's length from me, and I thought she was the saddest, sorriest sight I had ever seen. I tried to imagine how I might have felt, coming home from war a loser and finding someone I cared for in this state. The very thought made my heart ache and filled me with an unwanted sympathy for Orion Bell. I pushed it aside and put on my falsest grin.

"You are a vision, Ms. Bell," I said.

"You wear your uniform well, Mr. Kenning," she said with a delicate little curtsy, then swept past me and opened the front door. She lingered there for a moment and studied myself and the marshal. She seemed not to notice his shotgun at all. From within the house, I caught a whiff of rot and mildew. "Come along, gentlemen."

She went inside. We followed her.

4

The front door opened onto a grand foyer featuring a long, curving staircase and a dusty, lightless chandelier high above. Off to either side, open doorways led to long hallways lined with what looked like family portraits on the inner wall, and the front windows of the house on the outer. At the ends of those hallways lay closed doors, leading to who knew where. Beyond our immediate surroundings—the foyer, the staircase, the corridors leading to either wing and the gallery above— we could see absolutely nothing. The whole house existed in a permanent, Stygian darkness that only daylight—now almost fled—brought relief from.

Moreover, there was the very clear impression before the marshal and I of a home long abandoned, as though no attempts had been made to keep Bellhaven truly livable, truly energized by life and hope. Leaves, strands of grass, and dead weeds littered the foyer floor, cobwebs were apparent between the stair-rail posts, and every surface that we could see in the dying light—a writing desk, cushioned chairs, a bench, an end-table supporting a vase full of dead flowers—were all covered in many weeks-worth of dust.

Miss Livia Bell moved through this desolation without the slightest hint of shame or sadness. So far as she seemed to know, nothing had changed. Bellhaven was still the place that bore her, the comforting bosom that supported her, ever-ready to enfold her in loving arms and friendly shadows.

Something moved in a doorway beneath the staircase. I saw it first, but the marshal moved more quickly than I and raised his shotgun. "Who goes there?" he cried.

Livia Bell didn't seem to hear the desperation in his voice, or understand that one man was challenging another with mortal injury. Her bony face simply turned, slowly and calmly, toward the shadows moving in that open doorway, and peered into the gloom along with the pair of us, as if she, too, wondered just who else might be calling.

"It's us, sir," Mulvaney said from the shadows, then he and the corporal stepped forward. Mulvaney had his Colt Navy revolver drawn. The corporal carried a Spencer carbine. Both of them looked strangely relieved to be now emerging from the darkened recesses of the house, to once more be in the presence of their companions.

For the first time, I saw distress on Livia Bell's face. It was as though she could lie to herself about who I was, who the marshal was, but now, faced with the presence of the sergeant and the corporal, she could lie no longer. Our massed presence—three men in uniform and an officer of the law, all armed—created a clangor of discord that even the cacophony of her madness could not suppress. She studied us, each in turn, eyes darting between us, then she began to tremble. Her skeletal hands worked with the bundled wildflowers they held, crushing them, sending a storm of petals and leaves spiraling toward the detritus-littered floor.

"Who are you?" she asked. "I think there's been some mistake. I do believe—" she looked to me, and I saw something like fury and hatred in her eyes, "I do believe you lied to me, Mr. Kenning!"

"Do you see this uniform?" I asked, stepping toward her. "Do you see the insignia on my epaulets? What do they tell you? Who am I?"

She shook her head. Something in her didn't want to admit to who I was, or what I might be doing there. She dropped her wildflowers and pressed her hands to her temples. She began to shake as a child might, in the throes of a tantrum. "I don't know you," she said, again and again, "I don't know you and you shouldn't be here. You should go. Go. Now. He'll kill you if he finds you here!"

"Who?" I demanded, seizing upon this, her first inference of another who might share the house with her. "Who will kill us if he finds us here?"

I moved toward her. I didn't care if I threatened or frightened her any more. We'd come a long way. It was dark. We were in enemy territory and we had no more time for games with imbeciles or madwomen.

"Go," she said. "Go go go."

"Tell me," I demanded again, "who will kill us if he finds us here? Your brother? Your filthy, villainous, traitorous brother, Orion Bell?"

And then she lashed out at me. I believe it was the word 'traitor' that did it, for that was when she sprang forward, skeletal hands and ragged nails seeking my face, my eyes. She spewed forth an inhuman scream that sounded more like the bay of a hound than a woman's protest. The others lunged forward to my aid, but I caught Miss Livia Bell in my arms and held her close against me as she scratched and bit and kicked and beat at me and tried to cause me whatever pain she could. I felt her shaking, the tremors coming from deep within. I looked down into her big, dark eyes and saw the rage and the ruin hiding in the depths of them. She was more sane in those moments of trying to do me harm than she probably had been in years.

"Filthy, traitorous, nigger-loving, carpet-bagging blue-bellied scum of the earth!" she shrieked. "We should open all the doors and sweep clean all the thresholds of all the portals to all the storied realms and let the Outer Ones and the Elder Ones and the darkest night gaunts and the ageless shamblers have their infernal ways with the lot of you! You dare call my blood kin traitorous? You dare to come into my home in your blood-soaked, murderous blue uniforms! You little coots! You damned mudsills! You scabrous Sunday soldiers! You Jonahs!"

I was losing control of her. She managed to rake her filthy nails down one cheek. Had she aimed a little higher, she might have taken my eye. I turned, let Sergeant Mulvaney know with a look that I was done holding her, then thrust the sweet lady to the dusty floor, as roughly as I could. There was no honor left in me, no sentiment. I hoped to hell I hurt her. I wanted to see her whine and cry. I wanted her to bleed. I wanted to know just how deep her pain went and know that something I did had added to it.

Miss Livia Bell was on a tear, though. She hit the ground roughly, but immediately moved to regain her feet. The corporal stepped in then and leveled his carbine's fat barrel at her skull. He tapped her with it, just to make his point.

Livia Bell was still, but the murder never left her eyes.

"Now," I said, drawing my own enormous pistol, "let's get down to brass tacks, shall we, miss? Sergeant, get us some light before it's dark as the pit in here."

Sergeant Mulvaney assented and began searching the area for a lamp or candle. I knelt before Miss Bell, but kept my pistol where she could see it. She met my gaze with a murderous fervor. Truth be told, it made me nervous, for I could tell that however determined I was, she was more so.

The will of those people. By God, they would never bend!

"We're here for your brother, Orion Bell," I said flatly. "Tell us where to find him and you'll be left alone. No harm shall come to you, and no charges will be pressed."

She spat in my face. I wiped the phlegm away and drew a deep breath to keep myself calm. Nearby, I heard the scrape of a Lucifer match. Suddenly, a little light filled the great foyer. The sergeant had found a nub of tallow candle in a holder. He moved near to me, so that the light could fall on Miss Bell's wasted face.

"We've made quite a bit of noise and he hasn't shown himself," I said to her, "so I am assuming he's not here?"

"You'll never take him," Livia Bell said. "He can't be taken."

"Too fast and fleet for us cumbersome blue-bellies, eh?" I asked. "A regular Francis Marion for Calusa County?"

She smiled a little, then, a smile that was cadaverous and grave and sneeringly evil all at once. "The swamp's taken him," she said, "and he's taken the swamp. He is everywhere now. He's already surrounded you. You will never, ever see your home again, lieutenant."

I'd had enough. I snatched her up by one thin arm and threw her toward the marshal. She hit the wall near him and he stared at me, shocked at my sudden disregard for the woman's safety—or, apparently, my own sense of honor.

"Watch her," I said, then looked to the sergeant and the corporal. "The two of you, follow me."

We would take our single candle, and we would search that whole house top to bottom if need be. Clearly the woman's madness had returned. The swamp had taken him, he had taken the swamp… what did such nonsense even mean?

We began in the southern corridor of the foyer, following it all the way to the closed door at its end. We made no attempt at stealth. We simply approached the door, found it locked, then kicked it in. It took only two assaults, then yielded. Beyond, we found the inner sanctum of Orion Bell— the place where all of his evil and malice and blasphemous intentions were seeded and tended and brought to fruition.

The library.

I moved into the room slowly, taking it all in. Cherry-stained oak shelves stood floor-to-ceiling, crammed with leather-bound volumes of all sorts and varying ages. I was from a reading family, myself. I could only imagine the delight that myself or any of my kin could find in such a place as this. Books, floor to ceiling. Books on every wall. Books piled against the oak paneling and on every available surface. Hundreds. Thousands. More books than any one man or woman could read in a lifetime.

I searched the darkness around me for a lamp and found one. I lit it from the stub of candle in my hand, gave the candle to Sergeant Mulvaney, and moved toward the large desk on the far side of the room. It was strewn with papers and more strange volumes, some lying open, others in great, studious stacks. I moved nearer the desk and lowered the lamp in my hand to illuminate my discoveries.

The books that lay there were like nothing I had ever seen. The volume that happened to be lying open, for instance, contained pages of ancient and wrinkled parchment, the ink long-faded but still readable. In my life, I had seen and even learned to read a little Latin, and I knew well what Hebrew and Greek looked like, even with an untrained eye. But the letters and the language on those open parchment pages were like nothing I had ever encountered. Likewise, the strange illustrations and bizarre symbols that stood on the leaf adjacent to the writing. I couldn't guess what all that chicken-scratch meant, but my first inclination, upon studying its loathsome imagery and noting the age of the tome, was one of outrage. If, as Yates had suggested, Bell had undertaken blasphemous studies into the darkest of arts, here then were some of his text books. I looked to a nearby pile and studied some gilded titles on the leather spines visible: the nefarious *Book of Soyga*, the dread *Necronomicon*, a fiendish quarto titled *Liber Ivonis*, and what looked like a large ledger bearing the inky inscription *Los Testamentos de Porfirio Maldonado.*

Those were not tomes for idle study or light reading. Those dusty old volumes represented a doctoral education in blasphemy. While I had never read a one of them, I had heard them often alluded to—whispered of, decried—by the older students and professors of my ivy league alma mater back in Massachusetts. Law had been my chosen field of study, but there were more than a few odd an introspective loners and loonies at old Miskatonic that haunted the special collections and sought arcane knowledge from such moldy old tomes as these.

I remembered laughing at them along with my companions in those days.

And now, here I was, descending into a nightmare spawned from the pages of those same moldering, musty old books that I had once snickered at so derisively.

My God, what had we stumbled into?

"Sir?" Mulvaney said, as if trying to call me back from a subsuming reverie. He and the corporal had lingered by the door, not so curious about the contents of the room, and those books, as I was. When I turned to face him, Mulvaney moved slowly nearer. He saw the stack of strange texts before me and nodded the slightest. "Is it as Yates said?"

I nodded. "It would appear so."

"What do we do then, sir?" Mulvaney asked, and I couldn't quite tell if his knitted brows and pursed lips meant that he was eager for action, or eager to flee. Since he was just the non-com, he would, as was proper, follow my orders.

But what orders did he want me to give? What orders would see us all back to Tampa, to clean sheets, and warm beds? To another sunrise?

I never found my answer. Outside, someone cried in the night: Private Cabott. The cry was cut off by the sharp report of a rifle. The sound of screaming, neighing horses struggling against their reins followed.

Mulvaney and I rushed to the window. Before we had even reached it—before we even saw what I believe we each knew we would see—that witch, Livia Bell, was cackling away out in the foyer, laughing and laughing as though the most fabulous joke had just been played upon us.

The sergeant and I peered out of the library's front window. We saw a large body of men in white robes and white, peaked masks all lined up before the plantation house as though arrayed for muster. They had pistols, rifles, axes and pitchforks. Many carried torches, and the firelight made the front yard a bright and garish place, full of crimson light and deep black shadows. Private Cabott lay in the high grass beside the hitching post. I couldn't see the nature of his wound, but I could see the enormous, ever-expanding pool of blood that soaked the ground around him. I didn't think he would ever rise again.

I had no words. I felt sick to my stomach. I hated those men in their filthy white robes and masks almost as much as I hated myself. We were all about to die, and it was my fault.

Out in the foyer, Livia Bell kept cackling, taunting us. "Now, you'll learn!" she said. "Now, you'll learn and learn well! This is our land, Billy Yank! Our home! It was never yours and will never be—"

I heard the marshal curse at the woman, then came a sharp crack: wood against flesh and bone. I imagined the marshal had struck the woman with the butt of his shotgun.

One of the robed men outside stepped forward and called out to us. "We have the house surrounded! There's no way out for you! Come out, throw down your arms, and surrender, and you won't have to die here!"

I raised that big Walker Colt that I carried and cocked back the hammer. Beside me, Sergeant Mulvaney produced a second revolver—hidden all this time in the belt of his trousers—and with a pistol in each hand, cocked both hammers and spat.

Die here, they had said. That didn't bode well. That meant that even if we surrendered our arms, they'd probably just march us out into the swamps and lynch us. We'd die in the mosquito-infested mire of that bog just like the many negroes they'd murdered. I didn't fancy that as an end for myself. Given my druthers, a bullet sounded far more amenable than slowly choking while I danced a macabre jig at the end of a rope.

If I had to, I decided, I'd eat a bullet of my own, just like poor, mad Mr. Yates.

And I'd throttle that bastard when we met in hell.

Time to fortify. There were two doors into the library, on adjacent walls. The outer walls were thankfully short on windows—only one in each.

"Corporal!" I shouted, "Take up a position at that far door! Marshal! Bring us Miss Bell!"

The marshal answered with an affirmative and appeared a moment later, dragging the unconscious Livia Bell behind him. She babbled a little in her stupor, but otherwise she seemed out cold.

"That door is yours!" I said, indicating the door he stood in. "I think they'll be charging us. Put Miss Bell in the center of the room, by the desk."

"They might try to smoke us out," Mulvaney whispered.

"They might," I agreed. "But I think they would have tried that already if—"

I saw a knot of men come running up the walk and mount the stairs, all armed. They were sending their first party through the front door!

"Marshal, get ready!" I shouted, and hurried over to back him up. The marshal closed the library door part way. We had broken the lock when we kicked our way in, so there was no securing it except by barricade.

But before we barricaded it shut, we needed to take a few shots at our visitors.

Through the gap in the partially open door and its frame, I saw figures in white come swarming in through the front door at the far end of the front hall. The marshal raised his shotgun, took aim, and fired. A plume of smoke filled the hall and obscured my view, but I heard someone cry out in pain, then a heavy thump, as of a body falling. I tapped the marshal on the shoulder and he fell back. I took his place at the door, thrust my big Colt through, and took aim.

In the gloom, I saw white forms scurrying back and forth for cover. One of them stuck his head out from behind the door frame at the far end of the hall. I pulled the trigger. There was an ear-splitting roar and the white hood suddenly turned crimson. Down the bastard went without a sound.

Then they opened up on us. The marshal and I both hit the floor as a fusillade of buckshot and lead balls ripped through the library door. On our backs, we planted our feet against a three-tiered book shelf beside the door and pushed. The heavy shelf slid sideward, blocking the door. We shoved again and it pushed the door closed. The fire continued. Splinters and saw dust rained around us. Rounds punched through the book shelf we had used to barricade the door and some of the tomes came leaping off the shelves, torn paper and rent leather filling the air.

The men out front had opened fire as well. They had Sergeant Mulvaney pinned down behind a shelf, the front façade of the library wing providing better protection from low-grade fire than our door and plaster wall did. Nonetheless, their fire was heavy and more than a few rounds found weak spots in the architecture and punched right through. At a sudden break in their fire—probably so the shooters could reload—Mulvaney bounced up onto his feet, leveled his pistols, and fired out through the shattered window. He got off four shots before the fusillade began again. Some buckshot took him in the shoulder as he dove for cover.

I looked to the far door. The corporal had it slightly ajar, and was staring down the long back hallway that it connected to, his Spencer carbine at the ready. He was twenty-five years old, but looked like a scared and wide-eyed child.

"Is anyone coming?" I asked him.

He turned to look at me where I still lay on the floor. He opened his mouth to give me his answer.

Then a rifle shot tore a hole through his skull. I saw it plow into his left temple and send brain matter out his right. He collapsed without a word, mouth still open, about to speak. Cursing, I launched myself across the room, stumbling and half-crawling. When I reached his post, I snatched up his Spencer, took aim through the partially-opened door, and put a bullet in the first white robe I saw. A torrent of fire answered me. I threw myself out of its path, rolled over the dead corporal, and went crawling across the floor with the carbine toward the desk, toward Livia Bell—

—except Livia Bell was no longer at the desk. She was where I had just been, beside the marshal and the door from the front corridor. She had planted something long and sharp—a letter opener, I think—in the marshal's broad back. He was just toppling as she turned to face me, a satisfied, animal grin on her skeletal face.

I took aim with the carbine and put a round through one bulging brown eye. The bitch's damaged brain blew out the back of her head, taking a mess of mousy curls and intertwined wildflowers with it. I put another round in her as she fell, just for spite.

I heard boot heels out in the halls, fore and aft. Off to my right, Sergeant Mulvaney was cursing, trying desperately to open his pistols and change out their cartridges. He'd taken another shot in the volley. One ear was gone, blood pouring down his throat and congealing on his uniform collar.

"You're out?" I asked.

"Not for long," he said. "Just hold them off, sir."

I sat up and planted my back against the big mahogany desk. I had a good view of both doors. Already the front door was buckling, the bookshelf barricade about to give way to the press of bodies on the other side. At the rear door, the men were gathering and preparing to pour in, although they seemed more reticent, since they could not see what awaited them and had no barricade to wrestle with save the corporal's dead body.

I took aim at the back door with the carbine and waited.

One man threw the door open and rushed in. I shot him through the stomach and he doubled and fell. More men poured in behind him. I tried to shoot them as well, but the carbine came up empty. I threw it down and went for my holstered Walker Colt. Across the room, the barricade gave way and more men in white robes poured into the room.

Sergeant Mulvaney was fumbling with his gun cylinders, finding it hard to reload with shaking hands, a wounded shoulder and a bleeding ear.

I didn't know where to take aim, so I simply swung my arm back and forth. Cocked, fired. Cocked, fired. I think I hit two of them before they were on me. I cursed myself for not simply putting the gun in my mouth and pulling the trigger. I felt the flesh of the men who held me: it was chitinous and smooth, not human at all. I tore off at least two of their masks. The faces that stared down at me betrayed neither rage nor hatred. They simply stared, their eyes never blinking.

For a few moments, my whole world was a press of sweaty bodies in white robes, strange masks and blank faces, grasping hands and pile-driving rifle butts.

Then it was nothing at all.

I awoke with my head in a bag and my feet in deep water. I saw nothing, but I heard the murmur of voices, the sound of a strange, repetitive tattoo being beaten on a snare drum, and the sarabande of night winds swirling with serpentine grace through close-packed trees. I smelled fetid water, moss and mold, sweat, and the blood that had dried in my nostrils and on my swollen lip. I tried to move my hands but found my arms in the grip of powerful fists. Through the fibrous obstruction of the sack on my head, I could tell that we were in a very dark place, but that light was provided by torches.

The sack over my head was removed. The moment my eyes adjusted to the murky light and the deep shadows created by the flickering torches, I wished they had left it on.

We were in a watery glade, deep in the swamp, not unlike the ones I had imagined during Mr. Yates's tale of his time with Orion Bell. Cypress and pine surrounded us on all sides and we stood in two feet of brackish water. The glade was no longer just some darksome place tucked away from the civilized world—some little corner of a vast and largely untrod swamp made attractive by its very remoteness—but a temple, a decorated house of worship that threatened to make me violently ill. I shuddered to think what god held sway there.

Bodies—black bodies, for the most part—hung from the limbs of at least a dozen trees that surrounded us. They were in various states of decay, some clearly weeks old, a few perhaps as fresh as that night. They hung by their stretched necks, blue tongues lolling in black faces, a few eyes bulging from their sockets, many of their heads at unnatural angles suggesting that they were given the small blessing of a quick death by a broken neck, instead of slow strangulation. I counted two or three among them that had no faces any longer. My first thought was that the carrion birds had picked their flesh away. A moment later, when I studied the trees around me, I realized that carrion birds had not been responsible for those mutilations.

In addition to the many bodies swinging benignly in the breeze that combed the trees, there were also hundreds of faces—faces that had been cut from the bodies of the hung men and many more—stretched out grotesquely and nailed to all the tree trunks, like the vile wares of some hellish masquerade shop. Some of the faces nailed to the trees were white. The greater part of them were black. Lower to the ground, the swaying bodies and the flayed faces gave way to a loose ring of decapitated heads on makeshift pikes, ringing the central, watery clearing in the glade like the trophies of some savage huntsman in a faraway jungle.

But this was no faraway jungle. This was the United States of America, and all the heads and faces and hanged men that I saw surrounding me were hapless negroes, defiant farmers, and proud freedmen, all murdered in cold blood, dehumanized even beyond their murders, desecrated by their fellow countrymen like missionaries beset by cannibals in some godless jungle.

These were the people that I and my men were sent to Florida to protect from the likes of Orion Bell and his night riders. These were our charges… and we had clearly failed in our mission. Every flayed face glaring or screaming at me from the trees was a witness to my failure as a commander and as a servant of law and order.

All the men around me were dressed in white robes and masks, just as Yates had described. There was, truly, a religious air about the gathering, however blasphemous it might be. The tattoo beaten out by the drummer on his snare was clearly some sort of ritual invocation. As I studied my surroundings, all the men on hand began to moan and chant in unison, slowly joining in a song whose words I could not understand, but whose malign and alien intentions were all too clear.

What fate awaited me, then? Hanging? Would my face be nailed to one of these blasted trees around me? Or would they simply take my head and mount it on a pike as a trophy? Hell, I imagined they could do all three if they wished.

I just hoped I expired quickly when the bloody business began.

Then the swaying crowd of robed and masked men parted, and I saw something new: a man standing on a small, scrub-covered hammock that rose out of the black waters of the swamp. Before him lay the broad, flat stump of a tree, clearly felled in the near past, its remains now used as a sort of altar for the proceedings. This man wore no hood, but only a robe, and he stood with his arms out, his eyes closed, and his mouth busily reciting some strange prayers to the foul gods he intended to placate. I could not be sure, but I thought it safe to assume that the man I was now looking at was none other than Orion Bell, the scion of Bellhaven and the architect of all the evil unfolding around me. Had his bearing and place of influence not been enough of a clue, there was his superficial resemblance to the late and lunatic Livia Bell.

The drum beat lurched forward, picking up speed. The robed men all around me continued their strange, alien chant. The trees themselves seemed to creak and sway along with the movements of the supplicants, and behind the noise of the drums and the voices and the whispering wind, not a katydid trilled, not a bullfrog croaked.

Then they brought Sergeant Mulvaney to the hammock. He, too, had a sack over his head, but he struggled as they dragged him and lifted him up out of the water and onto the hammock's solid, mossy surface. Two men who stood near Orion Bell were close at hand, ready to take Sergeant Mulvaney from his captors and force him to lay down on the flat surface of the tree stump. Above the sound of the chanting voices and the snapping drum, I heard faintly the curses and invectives that poured out of Sergeant Mulvaney's mouth as he was forced by his captors onto his back. One man held his arms, another his ankles. Orion Bell opened his eyes and, never once letting his invocation falter, reached down and drew the sack off of Sergeant Mulvaney's head.

The sergeant, though clearly wounded and beaten after our volley with Bell's men at the plantation, still had a great deal of fight in him. Although my angle was an awkward one at which to see the proceedings, I could still see the flash of the sergeant's furious gaze, hear his curses spat from between clenched teeth, and see the way his body bucked and squirmed as Bell's men struggled to stretch him out. As the sergeant fought, Orion Bell reached under his robes and produced something new—a long, serrated knife made of some sort of chipped stone, like flint. The workmanship on the knife was primitive but elegant, and even from a distance I could see that the edge was sharp—razor sharp.

Sergeant Mulvaney tried to spit up into Orion Bell's face, but there was no saliva left in his mouth.

Orion Bell smiled—a mad and frightful grin that made me think of his insane sister—then lowered the flint knife and began sawing through Sergeant Mulvaney's throat. His intention was clearly to decapitate him, as slowly and painfully as possible.

Sergeant Mulvaney screamed. His body convulsed, his legs bucked and his arms tore against their bondage. His screams became wet gurgles. Finally, he could make no more sounds and his body was still. There was only the chanting of the crowd, the beating of the drum, the whispering of the wind in the trees.

Orion Bell lifted Sergeant Mulvaney's head high for all to see.

There was a loud report. The man who held my right arm pitched forward into the water, his head all but exploding in a shower of blood and brain matter and torn white cotton. The chanting around me stopped. The beating of the drums stopped. The man who held my left arm turned to scan the tree line.

That was my chance. I yanked free of my captor's grip—loosened for that moment of distraction—then threw all my weight against him. Down he went, sprawling, into the black water. Before anyone could react to my new-found freedom, before Orion Bell could give command or even understand what was happening, another shot rang out. A fellow in robes farther off to my left—who had apparently been lowering his rifle to draw a bead on me—moaned and sank into the water.

Someone was shooting from the tree line. They were trying to give me aid.

I rushed toward the trees. It was slow-going, trudging through that water and the uneven mud beneath, rife with roots and grasses and water weeds, but I decided then and there that, whoever was helping me, I would not hesitate or turn back. I would sooner be shot in the back and sucked down into those swamp waters than be lain on that altar stump and have my head sawed off like poor, defiant Sergeant Mulvaney. I would escape these devils or die trying.

And so, I fled. Within moments, I was trudging up onto hardwood hammock—onto dry and tangled surfaces where I could run and not be dragged to heel by the waters of the swamp. The moment I was up and out of the water, I ran.

I heard Bell behind me, crying out for his followers to give chase. I could not make out his words, but the anger and determination in them was apparent. He wanted me caught. He wanted me and whoever the mysterious person was in the swamp helping me brought back to him so that he could exact his revenge in ritual and see our bodies dedicated to his foul god—Nyarlathotep—or whomever, and know that our souls served his dread lord.

It wasn't long before I was in almost complete darkness, the torchlight from the temple in the pines falling far behind me and failing to penetrate deep into the swamp. I could barely see anything. My world was a rushing, roaring darkness smelling of mold and peat and damp earth and bearded moss. It was a world where I saw with my grasping hands, and heard with my stomping feet, and felt the sounds of my would-be captors' shouts and footfalls in my trembling bones. There was no moon. There were almost no stars. The canopy made by the cypress and the pines almost blocked out the sky entirely. I was blind and desperate, but I would not stop. I plunged on, doing my best to avoid the stray knees of cypress roots and clutching convocations of ferns and fetterbush. Somewhere behind me a rifle popped and something zipped past my right ear in the darkness. More shots rang out—rifles, pistols, shotguns. I heard ball and bearing nick bark and shred leaf around me. I knew that some of those shots came all too close to my soft, helpless flesh. But still, I ran.

Suddenly, someone collided with me in the dark. I thought at first it might have been an accident—one of my pursuers on a haphazard perpendicular trajectory, angling right into me and crashing bodily through the brush to tangle with me, limb and limb, until down we went. But when we both hit the forest floor and the other clamped his hand over my mouth and whispered in my ear, I feared something far more sinister.

"Lieutenant," he hissed, right into my ear. "It's me."

"Marshal," I croaked dumbly.

"They left me for dead," he said. "I have horses, but we have to hurry. Follow me and don't make a sound."

I raised my head to ask another question, but he shushed me. Then, he stood. He quickly cut back the way he had come, then fired two more rounds into the darkness, back toward our pursuers. Having drawn their fire one way, he then cut back in the opposite direction—back toward where I was just getting to my feet—then grabbed me by the arm and led me off into the swamp.

Little by little, we edged away from our pursuers. They were spreading out through the swamp, but we were moving on a line directly away from them, putting more distance between us and them with every passing moment. We darted through entangling pickerel and ferns, under drooping willow branches, through scrims of tattered Spanish moss and rushing soughs of cold, black water. After scrambling over half a dozen close-packed hammocks crowded with willow and pine, we finally reached a broad, more or less level area where the ground became very sandy and dry. Wiregrass and pine needles replaced ferns and fetterbush, and I saw three big forms in the darkness in a stand of maples.

Horses—one for the marshal, one for myself, one for the sergeant.

But, of course, the sergeant wouldn't be joining us.

The marshal helped me up into the saddle of one mount, then scrambled up onto his own. As he mounted, I peered off into the trees, back the way we had come. Far off—five hundred yards, a thousand—I could see the faint light of torches moving among the trees and scrub of the swamp like fireflies. I heard the calls of the men and their frantic attempts to surround and close us in. They had no idea we had already slipped them, that in moments, we would heel our mounts and we'd be off, heading back toward Tampa and safety.

But something caught my eye. In the darkness, among the trees, silhouetted by the torchlights moving in the distance, I saw what looked like a man. He stood alone and made no move toward us. His hands hung at his sides and he seemed to carry no weapons. For the most part, he seemed absolutely normal in shape and form, a figure cut in sharp relief out of solid darkness, a manikin made of night.

But as the torches all zigged and zagged in the distant woods behind him, I noted that there was something unnatural in his apparent form. It was as if wisps of darkness roiled and rippled off of him, like shifting shadows, with a curling, undulate quality that seemed like nothing less than roiling tendrils or grasping tentacles.

Likewise, his head seemed to stretch and curl unnaturally. It was as if his skull were made of smoke, and that smoke kept climbing, curling in on itself, skirling out on the breeze like a long and tapering banner.

And he was tall… so very, very tall. Perhaps seven or eight feet.

Or was that simply the distance between us? The shifting torchlight? The trembling shadows?

I blinked, trying to understand what I was seeing.

Then the marshal struck me, hard, apparently to get my attention. "Lieutenant!" he hissed. "It's time!"

I agreed. It was time.

We spurred our horses and high-tailed it out of there.

The marshal and I pressed our horses until they were foam-flecked and almost collapsed beneath us. I know not precisely how far we made it, but it had to be half a dozen miles, for when we stopped we were in sight of a broad but shallow stream that our party had passed early that morning when we first road into the area. We forded the stream, then dismounted and let our mounts rest on the far side. We kept an uneasy watch for the hour or so that we lingered there, talking little. Finally, we swung back into our saddles and rode on, keeping our horses at a canter, but not pushing them as hard as we first had. All along that tree-lined road through the wild darkness of Calusa County, we expected to be overtaken… to see men in a broad skirmish line across the road before us, or to hear the pounding of hooves and the thunder of guns from behind.

But it never came to pass. We rode on until daybreak, unmolested, then stopped in another nameless field to make a hasty camp and get some rest. As the first light of day appeared over the treetops, I told the marshal that I would take the first watch, that he could sleep soundly while I guarded him, since he had risked so much to save me. He was wide-eyed and hysterical—a state that had not been so apparent in the dark, when he played the role of savior and I of hapless victim—but at last, he seemed to calm himself and agreed to lay down. I did as I promised: I kept the watch while he slept.

The morning was uneventful. There were no pursuers forthcoming from the pine barrens that surrounded us, but I kept the watch as though they would show themselves at any moment. Long about noon, the marshal woke and offered to keep watch while I slept. I took him up on the offer and was just finding myself embraced by the arms of Morpheus when sudden thunder woke me. I sat bolt upright, awake in an instant, and saw that my companion had put both barrels of the loaded shotgun in his mouth and pulled the trigger. The thunder of the gun and the smell of blood had scared off the horses.

After that, I walked.

It was almost a week later when I finally came in sight of the rooftops and weedy lots of Tampa. For that interval, I had lived on grubs and raw corn stolen from barnyard cribs and the occasional snared bird. I'm sure I looked a fright, for when I tottered up to the barracks on uncertain legs, all the men came out to greet me, their eyes wide in disbelief, their mouths agape. The junior sergeant left behind to keep things in order while I and Mulvaney were away caught me when I collapsed. I half hoped, feeling the exhaustion of my body, the struggle that was every breath, and the sense of having finally made it home—or at least, back to a safe and secure clime—that that would be the end of me. I would—I could—die now, and die secure, without worry over the depredations of Dark Men or demons summoned with the aid of moldy old tomes. I slipped into unconsciousness, it was true . . . but I did not die. No, I simply slept for a week, lingering in a feverish daze as the local sawbones tried to revive me with tinctures and tonics, water and broth.

When I finally returned to the land of the living, fever conquered and consciousness restored, the young sergeant was waiting there at my bedside, eager for some explanation.

"What happened?" he asked. "Where are the others? What of Bellhaven and Yates's tales about Bell and his strange gods?"

"Let it lie," was the only reply I could manage.

That's precisely what we did. No inquiries were ever made. My official report said that my companions on that journey to lower Calusa County were all murdered by Confederate partisans still fighting the war they had, ostensibly, lost. While command wrote back, posturing on paper with a number of statements about how we would not—could not—stand for such open rebellion and brazen murderousness, the sad fact was that our time in Tampa was already nearing its end. It took only one more yellow fever outbreak to convince both my commanders and the people of the town that Tampa was done-for. In the spring of '69, the town council voted to disincorporate the city of Tampa. Soon after, we abandoned the place to the alligators and the mosquitoes.

Good riddance, I said. Good riddance, at last.

But the war was still not behind me. When I reached Tallahassee to rejoin command, I started scouring the newspapers for information on partisan activity in the other states. Tennessee, the Carolinas, Arkansas, Texas—they were all battlegrounds where unrepentant rebels used darkness and terror to wage their war on mankind and the Union. The president himself was said to be taking an interest in these nefarious guerilla wars, but the wheels of justice turned slowly in Washington D. C. My own inclination—so filled was I with a murderous rage and a despairing sense of helplessness—was to find my own means of prosecuting the war. It was the very least I owed my companions who never made it out of Calusa County. And besides, if one plantation prince could search moldly old books for the means to conjure allies from the ether—allies that could make of he and his men the savages that they were—who could say whether or not others, in separate climes, might undertake the same vile researches and come to the same damnable conclusions?

So far as I was concerned, any man who wore a mask and terrorized his neighbors and hung men from trees was just as guilty of consorting with devils and bestirring the dark powers of the world as Orion Bell.

I would go to where the violence was bloodiest, where the resistance ran deepest, I would cull out the men responsible, and I would personally murder them, one by one.

5

And that's precisely what I did, starting in Grantham, North Carolina. There, I culled out a winsome pair—both leaders in their respective Klan circles—and crucified them. One was nailed to a live oak, the other to a barn. From there, I drifted across the Piedmont, murdering, flaying, decapitating and making examples where I could, before finally pushing west into Tennessee and carrying on my nocturnal activities there. What I did was not done in the name of the United States government, nor goodness nor decency. It was not done for racial equality, nor for political gain. No, what I did was done in the name of rage, in the name of hatred, in the names of men I had served with who died horrid deaths at the hands of men in white robes, who prayed to vile gods. What I did was done in the name of terror and the name of revenge, pure and simple.

Thus, I fought a monstrous evil, and in the process, became a monster. That monster wore a man's face and manners and graces by day, but he was pitiless and spiteful and without humanity after the sun went down. That monster told himself he was serving a greater good by perpetuating his evils—told himself that two dead Klansmen here, four dead there, might tip the balance of power, might frighten more men into forsaking their masks and robes and terror and simply returning to their farms to live good, honest lives… but deep down, I knew the truth. I knew that every vile murder I perpetrated in the name of vengeance or justice was just food for something arcane and evil in my soul… that ultimately, I was serving nothing but my own rage, my own vanity.

The monster that I had become only admitted that he was a tool of evil, and no great bastion of good and justice, when he finally came into contact with the force that had yoked and used him.

This was in Little Rock, in about '74. I was in the back corner of a saloon one night, guzzling whiskey and enjoying a plate of beans and cornbread, contemplating my next foray—to crucify, to flay, or merely to dismember—when I suddenly heard music coming from the main room, and saw a strange pillar of light stab through the smoky darkness to illuminate a far wall. I rose from my table and moved on leaden feet around the corner of the small alcove I sat in, and found before me a grand, glowing image projected on the largest wall of the saloon, that wall now hung with an enormous white sheet.

It was a magic lantern show. As the images cascaded by—a Confederate private dead in a ditch, underfed Confederate soldiers with smoking pipes and dead men's stares around banked coals and shabby tents, Confederate dead littering a broad field under a sunny sky as far as the eye could see—I heard a woman begin to sing. She sang 'Dixie' in a slow and plaintive fashion, accompanied by an out of tune piano, a morose banjo, and a sighing harmonica. As her song and the images danced around one another slowly, funereally, I saw the roomful of patrons in that Little Rock saloon were held rapt. Many had tears in their eyes. More had murderous gazes and masks of pure hatred on their dirty, unshaven faces.

They were re-living the war, all over again.

I moved toward the magic lantern itself, and its operator, a tall man of dark complexion and regal bearing in a crimson suit. As I neared him, I could see that he seemed as taken with his own show as his patrons did. He whispered to himself in such a manner that those who sat closest to the magic lantern could hear him, his voice like the one in their own heads, no doubt, giving voice to their own bitter grievances.

"Those tyrannical sons of whores," the peddler muttered as he slowly, rhythmically changed the pictures in the aperture. "If only we could make each and every one of them—man, woman and child—pay for the blood they spilt… the bloody chaos they loosed…"

I recognized the voice, and its Shakespearean cadences. I also recognized his swarthy, old-world complexion and regal bearing. I should have felt some hatred, some loathing, some fury at this shameless profiteer's stirring up of old hatreds and old rivalries… some indignation in the shameless way that he worked his audience to pick at the scabs of their terror and loss, tugged at the strings of their weaknesses and prejudices.

But I could not summon fury at that moment. What I felt instead was a strange sort of wonder—a peculiar form of awe, as though coming into the presence of someone—or something—wholly alien, yet utterly, undeniably powerful.

And suddenly, I realized what a fool I had been. The monster could lie to itself no longer.

The peddler noticed me and smiled, as though delighted to come across an old, dear friend. "Lieutenant Kenning!" he said, and stepped away from his magic lantern to greet me. He took my hand in his and I felt my skin crawl when his flesh touched mine.

It felt strange. Chitinous and smooth instead of soft and supple. As he spoke to me, a rapacious grin on his face, his gaze never faltered, and his eyes never blinked.

"It's been an age," he said with a strange wistfulness.

"You," was all I could say.

"I've been traveling," he said. "Just as you have. Fanning the fires. Making sure that no one forgives and no one forgets. Amnesia is bad for business, after all."

"You," I said again.

"Oh, you're so shocked," he said, a little sadly. "You're all so, so, very shocked when you learn the truth. But honestly, why should you be? What difference does your indignation make in the grand scheme of things, eh?"

The image that he had left in the magic lantern lens began to bubble and smoke. It had been in the light too long. It was about to burn. None of the patrons seemed to care, though. It was a picture of Confederate dead stacked like cordwood. They were being administered to by negroes in Union uniforms.

"I was so very glad you made it out of the swamp," he said, leaning close and whispering in a conspiratorial manner that nearly made me ill—for I could smell the swamp he spoke of on his breath, in his clothes, the miasmatic foeter oozing off his chitinous skin like a vile cologne. "Honestly, I was quite sated at that point. And I had come to admire you. You were so very earnest and eager to do the right thing. I admire that."

"The swamp," I said dumbly, remembering our escape, and the tall, dark form that I saw among the trees, watching as we mounted and fled.

"That's why I kept watch," he said. "To make sure you made it safely away. And look at all the good work you've done in the interim."

The picture in the aperture of the magic lantern bubbled and burst into flames. The projection sheet went white. The people in the saloon all groaned a little, as though troubled by the absence of that most disturbing image that the peddler had left them with.

"Ah, duty calls," the peddler said. "But you, lieutenant, you are free. You can choose to abandon your good work any time you like. There will always be someone else eager and willing to do it for you."

The tall, dark peddler in the crimson suit hurried back to his magic lantern, to remove the burning picture from the aperture and resume his shadow show.

I left the saloon without a word. I left Little Rock within the hour. I left the South the following day.

And here I am, decades on, looking back and realizing what a fool I was—what fools we all were. The peddler's shadow show was always the same, his pitch as well—all that changed was his audience. And how eager we all were, from Maine to Mississippi, to keep fighting that war that we said was won and gone. In the end, I found it supremely ironic that we—the Union—beat the Rebels on the field of battle, then lost the war to them in towns and cities, in state legislatures and even in Congress. By 1890, the negroes we had fought to free and enfranchise were second-class citizens again, oppressed by the South and seen as an unfortunate embarrassment by the north. All that we had fought and bled and died for was nullified as a new season of legal oppression, enforced segregation, justified thievery, and institutionalized violence was inaugurated. Now, as an old man, I look around me and I see a house that has never been more divided against itself. One vile old codger here at the Soldiers' Home with me even received a post-card from a relation in the South that sported a photograph of some poor black man swaying dead at the end of a noose while a whole congregation of white faces looked on as though that poor, dead man were a prize buck downed by a local hunting legend.

In the end, I realize it has nothing to do with black and white, slave or free, Republic or Empire, monarch or serf, Christian or Moor, Egyptian or Jew, Viking or Saxon, Roman or Barbarian. No, the forces that sport with us and set us against one another and use us as weapons in the ongoing war that is the whole of human history—they don't care a whit what we fight for. They only care that we fight. We are the hornets, and they like to kick our nest and watch us whip ourselves into a frenzy and take out our fury on whatever poor, innocent soul chooses to pass us by at that moment—or, at the best of times, on one another.

I fought a monstrous evil, but in the end, I became a monster. We all became monsters. And worse, when we look in the mirror each day and see the monster, we are no longer frightened, or troubled, or repulsed. The monster has become our friend; his very fearsomeness and pitilessness fills us with pride. Murder is called justice, but really, it's only sport. We are like those tomcats I saw, tied tail to tail and dancing a bloody minuet as those slack-jawed, dull-eyed children from Orphea watched and made light of their cruelty.

I bought the peddler's wares. The price was my soul.

What, I wonder, will he barter from you when he comes to your town with his shadow show?

AFTERWARD

One writes with the door closed, then revises with the door wide open. Standing just outside that open door, offering support and guidance, were my most trusted readers: Matt Peters, Keith Gouveia and Mark Owens. Many thanks, amigos!

A historical note: while there are no records of local Klansmen worshiping Nyarlathotep or the Great Old Ones, it is a fact that Union soldiers occupied all the secessionist states and often fought bloody battles against deeply entrenched Confederate insurgents. It's also a fact that yellow fever outbreaks were endemic to the Tampa Bay area in the years during and following the Civil War, and that the city of Tampa was disincorporated in 1869.

Finally, I'd like to pay tribute to the man whose work provided primary inspiration for *No Surrender*: Howard Phillips Lovecraft, the single most important and influential writer of horror in the Twentieth Century, who died in poverty, thinking himself an abject failure. Even now, 75 years after his death, Lovecraft's work continues to inspire, entertain and stretch the boundaries of our collective imagination. If you've never encountered his work and you enjoyed *No Surrender*, I suggest you seek out the grand master's corpus forthwith. The former simply wouldn't exist without the latter.

Dale Lucas
August 30, 2013

ABOUT THE AUTHOR

Dale Lucas is a novelist, screenwriter, civil servant, and arm-chair historian. He is the author of the neo-noir Doc Voodoo series; the first novel is *Doc Voodoo: Aces & Eights* and the second in the series is *Doc Voodoo: Crossfire*. Dale's short stories have appeared in *Futuredaze: An Anthology of YA Science Fiction*, *Samsara: The Magazine of Suffering* and *Horror Garage*, and his film reviews in *The Orlando Sentinel*.

He lives in St Petersburg, Florida.

Find him online at:

www.facebook.com/AuthorDaleLucas

www.AuthorDaleLucas.Wordpress.com

@DaleLucas114 (Twitter)

DOC VOODOO
Aces & Eights

In *Aces & Eights*, Doc Voodoo races to uncover the source of a diabolical curse on a new Harlem nightclub. Navigating a minefield of gang rivalries, political corruption, and black magic, Doc Voodoo lays down a new law in Harlem, dispensing two-fisted justice with a heaping helping of hot lead!

Jam-packed with mobsters, mystery, magic and mayhem, Dale Lucas offers a love letter to classic pulp fiction like no other!

Available wherever books are sold!
E-book available at: Amazon.com, BarnesAndNoble.com, and
SmashWords.com